Sensorially Challenged

Volume 3

Copyright © 2021 Christopher Fielden. All rights reserved.

The copyright of each story published in this anthology remains with the author.

Cover copyright © 2021 David Fielden. All rights reserved.

Allen's Sensory Overload Writing Challenge was conceived by Allen Ashley.

Transcription and proofreading: Angela Googh

First published May 2021.

The rights of the writers of the short stories published in this anthology to be identified as the authors of their work has been asserted in accordance with the Copyright, Designs and Patents Act 1988.

All rights reserved. No part of this publication may be reproduced, stored in a retrieval system, or transmitted in any form by any means, electronic, mechanical, photocopying, recording or otherwise, without the prior permission of the publishers.

You can learn more about Allen's Sensory Overload Writing Challenge and many other writing challenges at:

www.christopherfielden.com

All characters in this publication are fictitious and any resemblance to real persons, living or dead, is purely coincidental.

ISBN: 9798728338819

DEDICATION

In memory of all those we have lost to COVID-19 over the past year. And a special dedication from Allen Ashley to his late friend, Jayne Buckland.

Chris Fielden and Allen Ashley, pictured at the British Fantasy Society Convention in Glasgow, October 2019

INTRODUCTION 1 – SENSORY SENSIBILITY

by Allen Ashley

Existing here on this Earth in physical form, we use our senses to help, ahem, make sense of the world around us. Sight tends to dominate, followed by auditory input. In other, non-human species, the sensory balance differs. Dogs have a highly developed sense of smell, bats use a sonar system of echo location and some snakes can detect heat. Not in our 'oh it's hotter than the Sahara / colder than the Arctic' manner but more along the lines of the infra-red images you might see on *Springwatch* or a true-crime investigation TV programme.

Far too many years ago, I read and reviewed a book set in early nineteenth century Tasmania, when most of the island was basically a prison colony. The opening line, setting the scene of disembarkation from the transportation ship as it pulled into the docks, has stayed with me ever since for its succinct scenic evocation. It read: 'Imagine the stench.'

As writers, we are often walking that tightrope between giving enough sensory information to make our locations and our characters real but also being careful not to come across like a garrulous estate agent after three bottles of Prosecco. Some of the favourite fictional locales of our age – Hogwarts, Middle Earth, Westeros – demand a certain amount of evocative description. And yet the Black Forest setting of many of the Brothers Grimm's fairy tales contains very little painting in of the scenery. What type of trees grow there? Firs, pines, oaks, conifers, fruit trees...? Somehow, the storytellers have conjured just enough for our imagination to fill out the arboreal gallery in our mind's eye. That's the key.

Writing this as the UK has just passed the year anniversary of the first lockdown, it is clear that we have all experienced an amount of sensory deprivation during the pandemic. This is often characterised by the shorthand questions of: When will it be safe again to hug our grandchildren or grandparents; or even just to shake hands with a friend or colleague? We have all been feeling somewhat out of touch.

So, this anthology feels particularly pertinent right now. A celebration of the senses. Something that makes us human.

Allen Ashley
London, March 2021

INTRODUCTION 2 – SENSORIALLY SATIATED

by Chris Fielden

Welcome to the third sensory challenge anthology. This is the fifteenth book published via the writing challenges run on my website.

Here's a brief history of the sensory challenge:

- Autumn 2016: Allen and Chris met up in Bristol, had a few beers and then the rest of this brief history began to unfold because it seemed like a good idea after a kebab (incidentally, kebabs impact *all* of the senses [not always in a good way, unless you're inebriated, when they transform into a divine source of nourishment])
- March 2017: Allen's Sensory Overload Writing Challenge unleashed
- August 2017: 100th sensorially saturated story received
- December 2017: *Sensorially Challenged Volume 1* published
- January 2019: 200th sensorially overloaded story received
- June 2019: *Sensorially Challenged Volume 2* published
- February 2021: 300th sensorially encumbered story received
- May 2021: *Sensorially Challenged Volume 3* published

Volume 4 is already filling up, but it will be a little different to the other books published in this series because it will contain 200 stories by 200 authors.

This is for a variety of reasons, which include making

my workload more manageable and having more authors in the book. Here's an explanatory equation to add clarity to the latter:

>100 x A* *(should)* = >S** + >CotBBaB*** + >M£fC****

I'm not sure that's made anything any clearer... Can you tell I'm not a mathematician? Us drummers only know the important numbers: 1, 2, 3, 4 and more.

Anyway... an extra 100 authors *should* result in more sales, a better chance of the book becoming a bestseller and more cash for charity. If this goes as we hope, we can all herald the plan (and my equation) as a gloriously purple, aromatic, rough, delicious and noisy delight.

We'll see if it works when it happens (I used to err on the side of caution and put 'if/when' in sentences like this, but have stopped that practice as these books always fill up eventually, even when they have 1,000 authors in them, so I can say with confidence that *Sensorially Challenged Volume 4* will be no exception).

That's enough waffle from me.

The stories in this book are presented in the order they were received. Proceeds from book sales support the National Literacy Trust. I hope you enjoy reading the stories as much as Allen and I have enjoyed presenting them in this collection. Over and out.

Chris Fielden
Portishead, March 2021

* authors
** sales
*** chance of the book being a bestseller
**** more money for charity

INTRODUCTION 3

by The National Literacy Trust

The National Literacy Trust is a charity dedicated to raising literacy levels across the UK, working to improve the reading, writing, speaking and listening skills in the UK's most disadvantaged communities, where one in three people have low levels of literacy, which can hold them back at every stage of their life.

When children enjoy reading and writing it has a transformative impact on how well they do in school and in every aspect of their future lives. We are so grateful to the editors, authors and readers of this anthology, whose passion and support will help us to change life stories by giving even more children a route out of poverty.

To find out more about our work, please visit:
www.literacytrust.org.uk

ACKNOWLEDGMENTS

Big thanks to Allen Ashley for conceiving and helping me bring the Sensory Challenge to life. You can learn more about Allen here: www.allenashley.com

Thanks to David Fielden for designing the cover of this book and building and maintaining my website. Without him, I'd never have created a platform that allowed the writing challenges I run to be so successful. You can learn more about Dave's website building skills at: www.bluetree.co.uk

Thank you to Angela Googh for her help preparing the interior of this book.

Finally, a delicious, colourful, velvety, pungent and, most importantly, very loud, "THANK YOU," to everyone who has submitted their stories, supported this sensational idea and, in turn, raised funds for the National Literacy Trust. Without the support of all the writers who submit their stories, this simply wouldn't be possible.

SENSORIALLY CHALLENGED

201: TANKED UP

by Allen Ashley

Martin likes being inside his tank of smart liquid; but I hate the confinement.

"What sort of life is this?" I moan. "I feel really out of touch."

"For the hundredth time, Simon, the whole point of sensory deprivation is to free the mind to think, to wander, to transcend."

"But all it's doing is making me miss a whole gamut. The smell of Janine's perfume; the salty taste of crisp bacon; the uplifting strings of a Mozart symphony; the touch of silk or cashmere against—"

"Yeah, I know, pal. And watching the sunset. Give it a rest, right? They're all gone."

It's true. I don't have a mouth or ears anymore. All this talking is happening telepathically. I can't see Martin, either. But I know he's there: another bodiless brain preserved in a glass jar.

Occasionally, I reach out mentally to the other unlucky survivors. I'm losing my sense of time here. We're all lined up in Perspex rows in the dark. Missing the touch of skin, the taste of coffee...

Forever.

Allen Ashley's Biography

Allen Ashley is the co-originator of the Sensory Challenge. His latest book is the poetry collection *Echoes from an Expired Earth* (Demain Publishing, 2020). He is President of the British Fantasy Society.
   www.allenashley.com

202: MORNING TEA

by Sarah Williams

Moving through the dawn-cold kitchen with half-sleep muscle memory, she found the tea caddy. The kettle was placed over the orange flame and the heating water began knocking against its metal sides.

Her hand dipped into the tin and her fingers found the papery cocoon of the tea bag. It felt warm, dry and almost like skin, encouraging her thumb to move back and forth across its surface.

Absentmindedly, she brushed it against her lower lip. She inhaled the smell of Christmas and Indian chai tea. First the warm smell of cinnamon, then the sharp, antiseptic, nostril numbing clove.

The kitchen window sweated with steam. She watched the larger drops combining, producing little tear rivers running down the glass.

The kettle began to demand attention. She went to it before the whistle squealed its top note.

The hot water hit the teabag, which started to bleed sepia into the filling cup.

There was a pause, the chinkle, chickle of the spoon.

Then the first sip and sigh of the day.

Sarah Williams' Biography

Sarah is 53, an artist and entrepreneur who appreciates the few moments of thoughtfulness that the first cup of tea of the day brings.

203: CAFFEINATED COGNITION

by Shay Meinecke

Bass and treble buzz around me in a hipster cafe as I order a black, pungent filter coffee from a nose-pierced, tatted blonde, who looks more like a punk singer than an overworked barista.

I stand to the side of the sleek, wooden high-top bar and eavesdrop on a hushed conversation from two energetic girls sitting nearby.

One of them, toned with deep wrinkles and a pale face, chats with a heavier-set friend in a language I barely understand. "This and that," I presume she says, "with the guys and girls," she continues, "we went there and did that," she finishes. Her friend with rosy red cheeks and dark, bushy eyebrows laughs and snorts between lusty bites of a Danish apple pastry that makes me sort-of chuckle.

I receive the piping hot cardboard cup and find a seat by a frosted window in hopes of catching some warm sun before it sets behind the white winter mountains.

I sip the earthy, aromatic java as my bottom numbs and my heart races.

Shay Meinecke's Biography

Shay Meinecke is a US-born journalist for Germany's international broadcaster, Deutsche Welle, and was previously a travel TV reporter for South Korea's global broadcaster, Arirang TV. He's been to 30-plus countries and hopes to publish 30-plus stories.

www.shaymeinecke.com

204: TASTE THE MUSIC

by Christopher Fielden

I'm sweating, captivated by the frenzy of a beat so powerful it sounds like a living, breathing monster. The rhythm section motor behind me, smoke clouds the air and the stage lights burn.

The atmosphere is vibrant, the crowd hungry. Ian Maiden's bass rumbles with wrath. Jack Sabbath unleashes a demonic riff. Beneath my feet, I feel the stage throb with the thrum of music. A mass of bodies bounce before me in unison.

Dwight Snake points back at me and shouts, "You wanna hear some guitar?"

The crowd roar.

"You asked for it, you metal maniacs. I give you, Dave,

"Against,

"The,

"Machiiiiiiine."

I face my wall of Marshalls and allow the hum of feedback to grow. The volume becomes painful before I turn to face the audience, unleashing a solo that feels as though it's oozing from my fingertips rather than me having to play it. As I hold the final note and push down hard on my Les Paul's whammy bar, Dwight starts hollering lyrics.

The show begins.

Christopher Fielden's Biography

Chris writes, runs a humorous short story competition, plays drums and rides his motorcycle, sometimes to Hull and back again. He runs a multitude of writing challenges and has published 1,000s of authors in support of charity.

www.christopherfielden.com

205: GOODBYE ROGER

by John Rivers

"Why would I agree to that?" The earlier argument with Roger shot round Laura's head, as she collected her rubbish bin from the street. The very *idea* of making someone 'disappear'. No trace. Cover my tracks. All for love and £250,000 insurance.

A blue sports car briskly parked. Nervously, Laura looked. It was Roger.

Stepping out he hissed, "Well?" in greeting. "Are you in? Be a decoy. Easy."

Clang. Laura dropped the dustbin. The plan was terrifying, yet thrilling. Roger was persuasive. She loved him. Her husband, Paul, was boring. A selfish, rich bully. He knew nothing of Laura's affair.

She was rough, pushing past Roger, to pick up the bin.

"OK," she muttered.

"Sweet," said Roger, striding to his car. "I knew you'd agree."

Paul appeared, walking on crutches from an unexplained mishap. Near the primroses at their gate, Laura took his arm, curiously saying, "I'll help you cross the road."

With Paul in view, Roger accelerated hard from his parking spot.

He didn't see the truck pull out 'til too late.

VOLUME 3

John Rivers' Biography

John Rivers works as a classical musician and teacher, maintaining a freelance career. As a home husband, he has gained an unexpected interest in growing vegetables – acquired from his wife – and constantly reads all manner of books.

206: EUTOPIA

by Lesley Anne Truchet

The warmth caresses my nakedness. Liquid heat seeps through my body, extending to every extremity. Relaxed, I stretch cat-like and sigh with pleasure. Seagulls caw in quadraphonic harmony and the *shhhh, shhhh, shhhh* of the lapping waves on the sea shore act like a lullaby. Is that the scent of rotting seaweed invading my nostrils? Maybe. My eyes are closed in bliss and I can almost taste the salt of the ocean.

A hand creeps from my towel. I want to feel the sand oozing between my fingers. Eyes still shut, I touch – empty space? I'm thrown back into reality. Crawling out from under the sun bed, I look out at the pouring rain, turn off the ocean sounds mood music and prepare to leave for work.

Lesley Anne Truchet's Biography

Lesley Truchet has been writing for several years and has a number of short stories, articles and poems published on paper and on the internet. She is currently writing her first novel.

207: TAKING A PART

by Michael Rumsey

Amanda, darling. Your email spread a warm joy upon seeing it – such a delight to hear from you.

Exciting news. I have a whiff of a new play in the West End. Auditions on the 16th. Yes I know, dear, me doing auditions when just a glance at my CV sends one into raptures, but it's the producer. Archie Armstrong no less. Yes, him of the flowery prose and nose.

Remember when we did the open air theatre summer season with him? A breath of fresh air, we thought. Huh, how very un-refreshing his pipe smoke turned out. And then that rumour about him touching up young Margie...

But needs must, sweetie, and how marvellous it is to be at the Argon Theatre. I faint every time I see it, with its delicious aroma and divine acoustics. In my heart, I know I shall take a part.

Do come to opening night. I long to set eyes on you again and drown once more in your dulcet tones.

Love, kisses and caresses. Randy.

Michael Rumsey's Biography

Michael spent a large part of his working life travelling, first with the RAF and later in international business. It gave him writing opportunities and he's been published in four different countries. Now retired in Athens, he concentrates on flash fiction.

www.facebook.com/mrumsey

208: WAITING

by Robert Pembroke

He looks up when the tangy aroma of vinegar reaches his nostrils, making his mouth water, and he can almost taste those fried potatoes. People mill around in front of him, but he picks out the person with the bag of chips and stares longingly.

A group of school children come down the stairs, their blue and red uniforms looking bright in the late afternoon sunlight. There is the chatter of people standing around him. While some talk into mobile phones, overhead there are train announcements being made. This hustle and bustle doesn't bother him, because he does this journey nearly every day. Then he hears it. The train approaches, its steel wheels screeching noisily as it pulls into the platform.

Just then, he feels the harness handle being lifted from his back and the hand ruffles his fur as, once more, he is standing ready to guide his master onto the train, the train which will take them home where a well-earned dinner awaits.

Robert Pembroke's Biography

I'm 64 years old, totally blind and I'm self-employed as a therapist. I live in Dagenham with my wife, Jan.
www.rsptherapies.co.uk

209: IN THE SOUP

by David McTigue

Ben couldn't believe his eyes. 'Bacon Causes Cancer' screamed the headline on his laptop. He laughed and turned to the pan of lamb broth on the hob.

"More salt," he decided, taking a slurp. "Ow, that's hot."

Ben loved cooking, particularly when alone, listening to classical music. It would finish before Shirley got home. Not a fan of Beethoven, our Shirl. She'd come in, a wall of sound, complaining about her supervisor, Megs, or Dregs as Ben called her.

The doorbell shrilled.

Damn. Sheila. His mother-in-law.

He let her in. Sheila breezed through.

"Mmm, something smells nice and sounds awful," she chimed, instinctively picking up a spoon.

"No," Ben admonished. "Too many cooks and all that. Bacon sandwich, Sheila?"

She shook her head. "Where's Shirley?"

Almost on cue Shirley walked in. "Hello, love," she said, "Oh, hi Mum, I've had a brilliant day. Meg's off."

The rest of the conversation melded into the background as Ben tested the broth. Off? Not off at all. Megs Lamb was still very fresh.

David McTigue's Biography

Lives on outskirts of Liverpool. Married, three kids, one grandson (so far). Published in various magazines and local free press in the dim and distant. Enjoying getting back into the writing swing, Muse permitting.

210: PUB AT SEVEN

by Sean Bain

"And a bottle of coke with a straw and some salt and vinegar crisps."

Yes, music to my ears, but the pong of beer and fags attacks my nose. So I'm off, like Batman to the Batslide. I gawp mesmerised by its shiny, silvery... slideyness?

Clamber those splintery steps, reach the two metre peak and touch the sun.

I hear the fizz from the bottle whilst my mouth chases the straw. *Sluuurrrpp.* More energy required. Crisps. *Oh my god, they're like radioactive bits of crunch.* My eyes water and my cheeks collapse. Now it's time to WHEEEEE. Again and again. I am a giggle machine.

I shimmy down once more, ignoring the hot summer heat, metal burning my legs. My plimsolls squeak on metal.

Racing around the grass with that 'just cut' aroma.

Squelch. So soft.

"Eurghhh." That's not grass. I clasp my nose, staring at the black and brown foot.

"Don't you dare," Dad scolds

The slide whispers, "One more go."

Decisions, decisions.

Sean Bain's Biography

My name is Sean. I am 48 and rapidly approaching my teens. This is my second challenge on Chris' site and I am now enrolled in his comprehensive course. I suggest you do the same. Why wouldn't you?

211: LEVEL CROSSING

by Sue Partridge

The train suddenly lurched and, with a screech, came to a halt. June wiped her hand along the cold window, making a small spy hole through which she caught sight of a blue van rolling over and over in the adjacent field.

Alarms on the train started to ring and, with a loud clang, the driver's door flew open. The uniformed man leapt out of his cab into the rough grass and raced towards the van. As he approached, a figure crawled out of the wrecked vehicle and slowly got to his feet.

"Are you OK?" shouted the train driver.

"Yes, I'm fine," came an unsteady reply, "but my van isn't."

A faint, sweet aroma wafted in the air as the dishevelled man rubbed his head and looked down at the tangled heap of metal that was his van.

"And I think that's the end of Primrose Pies too."

Sue Partridge's Biography

I am a retired finance officer, enjoying a new lease of life. I play violin in a quartet, I am learning jazz piano and I have just started to discover the art of writing.

212: MEET THE PARENTS

by Paul Mastaglio

Sam turned to Jackie exclaiming, "Don't look at me like that. Not with those blue eyes. P-please."

"Why, they're the only ones I've got," she laughed.

"I'm done for then. I can't say no."

Jackie grinned. "Off to meet Mum and Dad we go then."

Ten minutes later and Jackie rapped on the door knocker, making a large clang.

"Mum."

"Come in, my dears, come in."

Wiping their feet on the rough mat, in they went. Soon, they were in the living room and being introduced to Jackie's dad, Tom Burns.

"Would you like some of my sweets?" he enthused. "Absolutely delicious. Try some."

"Hmmm," they chorused.

Jackie's mum, Heather, followed them in. "Cup of tea, anyone?"

"No thanks, Mum. Mum, Dad. Please sit down. We've got something important to tell you."

It was suddenly very hot in the room. Jackie opened a window, ushering in cool, fresh air with a scent of primrose from the garden.

"We're engaged," she blurted out. "This is my fiancé, Samantha Daniels."

You could hear a pin drop.

Paul Mastaglio's Biography

I'm a retired bank clerk who lives with my wife, Yvonne, in North Tyneside. Interests include archery, reading and making attempts at writing.

213: MY RESIGNATION LETTER

by K. J. Watson

Dear Mr Hardiman,

Today, I began my calls to the homes on your list.

I made only one visit and should probably have left when I reached the front garden. A mess of split bin bags and indecent-looking ooze belaboured my eyes. A second later, an odour from what I imagine might come from a pit of plague victims assaulted my nose. Acidic bile rose in my throat and coursed across my tongue like demonic mouthwash.

I persevered, though. A shiny door knocker lay ahead. I grasped the knocker and, too late, realised that it was thick with metal polish. Stinging gobbets of the stuff clung to my fingers.

I was trying to clean my fingers on the roughcast wall of the house when the door opened. A smiling, elderly lady greeted me. For a moment, her presence calmed my distraught senses. Then, behind her, an enormous dog barked thunderously, ripping the fabric of my eardrums. I hastily retreated.

I must therefore tender my resignation. I believe that I'm too sensitive to be a bailiff.

K. J. Watson's Biography

I am a copy editor and online content writer. My occasional fiction includes scripts for a comic and annual (some while ago) and stories for young children. I live near Loch Lomond with my wife and two dogs.

214: WINNER

by Mike Scott Thomson

On this blizzard-white sheet of paper are six stupefying squiggles in ebony ink. (Confusion kicks of coal, compounded with cantaloupe; frustration festers like fresh fertiliser.)

The index finger of my left hand traces the outline of the first hieroglyph: an impassable mountain between two fathomless valleys.

The next, a blazing black sun hovering serenely over a lamppost.

(Was that an 'i'? For 'ischaemic'? An unwelcome addition to my lexicon. All others took their leave to the thunderclap of tarmac, the tang of red-hot chilli sirens, the lavender fragrance of flashing lights... memories, the twinkling of piccolo and a booming of bass... the written word, alphabet soup. The night my senses scrambled.)

I rustle the paper. (A chirp of cicadas.)

One. Mountain. Two. Lamppost.

The third and fourth symbols are identical: twin hillocks in an autumn meadow.

The fifth, a slippery, squashed spiral.

But with the sixth, I turn a corner.

I trace them again. The contours click-clack into familiar form.

I understand.

I smile.

There was only ever going to be one.

Mike Scott Thomson's Biography

Mike Scott Thomson's short stories have been published by journals and anthologies, plus have won the occasional award, including first prize in Chris Fielden's inaugural To Hull And Back competition. He lives in south London.

www.mikescottthomson.com

215: JOIN THE ARMY: JOBS FOR DRIVERS ALWAYS AVAILABLE

by James Louis Peel

Bright blue-eyed Corporal Laika braced herself too late. The jolt of the fiery blast ripped hard through the personnel carrier, sending so much twisted pain into her guts that she decided it best to drop out of this overly glorious line of soldierly work.

Her sixth sense and training kicked in, comforting her so at least she would not taste the bile and choking fear. She tumbled freely around in the salty stench of fresh guts and hot metal. Her mind recoiled and her ears rung.

"To hell with them – drive on," Sergeant screamed.

Events played out in grimy, bright detail. And yes, there was nothing she could do. The government-issued green band of her watch snapped, spinning like a touching ballerina through space. Watching it felt like five godless eternities.

A bright idea flashed: *Jump from the APC.*

Too late.

She never felt the second impact.

Corporal Laika's blue eyes were sightlessly open as the busted engine began to hiss.

James Louis Peel's Biography

From Kentucky, James now lives and works in Japan. Stories in English are the lifeline to his sanity. The rest of the time, he can be found babbling in Japanese with workmates in the ever changing world of business.

216: REMEMBERING IS THE KEY

by Maggie Elliott

Perched on a stool, amid garden tools and cultivating seeds, I realise ventilated footwear wasn't a shrewd move.

Boulder-like raindrops pummelled my hair, which now hangs limp.

Magazines and lottery tickets merge in my shopper, producing a kaleidoscope of colours.

Glancing towards home, felines watch me watching them and I detect smugness.

I alleviate boredom by calling my son but don't reveal my predicament. Goodbye reminds me little time has elapsed.

The stool shakes as my body objects to saturated clothing adhered to it. Tissues disintegrated, I consider using my sleeve to wipe my nose but realise the futility and resist.

Battering rain intensifies my feeling of misery until I remember my phone is brimming with soothing music.

Later, my partner slides the greenhouse door open and asks, "What're you doing in here?" My scornful look elicits a response of, "Forget your keys?"

The absurdity forces me to ignore him and squelch my way indoors.

My body tingles as warmth envelops me and I chastise myself for being absentminded again.

Maggie Elliott's Biography

Maggie writes for pleasure since retiring. Her poem 'Picture Me Calm' won third prize in the *Writing Magazine* poetry competition June 2017. She has three stories published in anthologies and more pending.

217: SAFE

by Huguette Van Akkeren

The pungent, briny aroma assaulted her with each short, sharp breath. Fear pulsated through her small body, propelling her into the foetid, tropical swamp. The tepid afternoon breeze barely cooled her sweating arms, as disturbed mosquitos swarmed their first prey.

Staggering barefoot through the scorching soft sand toward the dilapidated waterfront fishing hut was torture. Sand-flies crawled unabated on exposed sections of leg. Perspiration slid down her back, causing the dirty cotton shirt to stick uncomfortably. Terror fuelled body odour added to the malodorous aroma permeating the raised winding pathway.

Slitherings and slidings, rustlings, creaks and croaks, the ominous sounds sharpening her awareness that things she would prefer not to encounter resided less than a metre away in the dense scrub. Her parched mouth and dry cracked lips begged for water, but still she ran.

The flashing red and blue lights blinded her as she burst into the small clearing, straight into the arms of the surprised yellow-clad volunteer.

"You're safe now."

Relief flooded the exhausted child's senses as she was lifted into the ambulance.

Huguette Van Akkeren's Biography

I was a retiree. Now I'm an aspiring writer and student who loves challenges and useful feedback to help further my dreams of one day publishing a novel.

218: WALKING THE DOG

by Scott Parent

It's still dark and only 33 degrees outside. Large, slushy raindrops darken the street lights. They beat hard on the windows, each ending with a slushy splat.

I harness the dog and go out into the cold winter morning. An icy wind stings my face. After a couple of moments, I can barely move the muscles of my mouth and nose, which is dripping onto my upper lip. It tastes of cold and salt.

The rain finds its way onto the back of my neck. Wet gloves steal the feeling from my fingers and replace it with a cold, stinging sensation. My shoes and socks are getting wet and cold from stepping in puddles of slush. I can't feel my toes.

Still we trudge on, hunched forward against the wind.

Scott Parent's Biography

Born in Massachusetts, Scott Parent earned his graduate and undergraduate degrees from Worcester State University. In 1992, he moved to North Carolina to take a teaching position. He's been writing on and off most of his life, though never professionally.

219: SLIDING DOORS

by Josh Granville

I took my glasses off in calculation, before tucking them into the inside lining of my blazer, the newspaper exiting at force before my feet bounced off the surface of the platform in acceleration.

It was all or nothing now. Bashing against businessmen's briefcases, I dodged past the customers at the Greggs kiosk in a timely, cautious manoeuvre, the burning of sausage rolls wafting through the station.

Breathing heavily, the announcer's whiffy breath exhaled onto the whistle, bubblegum popping against the loud speaker in a piercing yet tense intrusion, his lips lingering as he looked towards the last carriage. Then he blew. That was it, no more time. The doors started moving; five high-pitched beeps screeched in quick succession as they attempted to re-unite. Heads shifted towards me as I leaped over the yellow line. Reaching out promisingly, my fingers attempted to wedge in-between the ever-narrowing gap. Then the noise stopped. A spilt second. I pushed with all my weight.

Relief. I was on.

Josh Granville's Biography

I am a young, creatively driven writer with a flair for words and waffling. I like to create humour and meaning through a play on words and experimentation.

220: THE HUNTER

by Aleksandra Petrovic

I stepped in anxiously and the wet earth seeped in-between my toes like a birthday cake in a greedy child's hands. The scent of mud rose through the air, cut through by a refreshing smell of cold water.

"Just a little more," shouted my aunt above the noise of the stream. "Over here are plenty of them."

A shudder zipped up my spine as my feet reached the rushing waters, the swept-up mud tickling away at my soles.

"Now," she called.

I hurled the line and observed it fall into a sparkling patch of water, narrowly avoiding a small nearby whirlpool, which they would avoid.

Soon enough, I felt a tug and I pulled on my trembling fishing rod. A shot of silver streamed through the air like a comet in reverse and it fell on the grassy banks. I hurriedly waded to the shore, where my prey gave itself away by flipping on the green. The fish twitched in my hand as I removed the hook.

Salty fried minnows for dinner. Delicious.

Aleksandra Petrovic's Biography

Aleksandra Petrovic was born in Serbia and raised on the sunny island of Cyprus. Obtaining her Bachelor and Master's degrees in London, she has since worked in a number of countries in Europe and is currently residing in Barcelona.

221: REVELATION

by T. J. Hobbs

"Why did I agree to that?" Pete whines like a child.

I look at him as it hits me like a sledgehammer. *I no longer love him.* Immediately, I feel a huge weight has lifted from my heart at this revelation. My body shudders as the tension I've been holding onto for so long is released.

I take a deep breath of tangy sea air and lick the salt off my lips, feeling the Earth's energy surging up through me like it had once before. I look out into the azure sky, over the white waves crashing onto the silver beach and know there's a huge smile on my face.

I turn to him and say, "I really don't care what you do any more, Pete. I'm leaving."

His mouth drops open in surprise as I normally give in to him, but not anymore. I walk past him towards my primrose yellow car, to the freedom I have given up for far too long.

T. J. Hobbs' Biography

I'm a published author of three spiritually themed novels, living and working as a natural healthcare practitioner in Hampshire. I love writing as well as travelling, photography, horses and nature conservation as a volunteer with BCV.

222: TASTE, THE EVILEST OF SENSES

by Victoria Mason

My mouth opens and fills with saliva as my sunken eyes scan the shiny laminate menu that is fastened to crumbling plasterboard behind Nora, the proprietor.

"There are other customers besides you, Bill," she spits, her green eyes looking me up and down suspiciously. "Didn't think you were the sporty type," she adds smugly.

*

My enormous frame moves around, like a half-deflated beach ball, within the white plastic chair. I pick at a bit of dried tomato sauce that is attached to the table and breathe in deeply. I smell the bacon and imagine chewing the caramelised fat. Golden butter sparkles in the fluorescent lighting, sinking further into white sliced bread. Two identical sausages glisten and glide effortlessly as I push them away with my fork.

My bouncing belly longs for the food, growling like a child, telling me it doesn't like quinoa.

I draw a stick man in the condensation of the dripping window. While lifting myself up, I groan, thinking of the treadmill, and plod out the door.

Victoria Mason's Biography

When I am not writing or playing the banjo, I am a chef. I have recently moved from England to New Zealand with my Kiwi husband. I have been writing stories for a couple of years.

223: SHOWDOWN

by J. S. Wellian

Long awaited scrumptious revenge is approaching. Soft, sweet Arnold against spoilt-rotten James.

The bell rings. *Thud.* Arnold gets up. *Splat.* Arnold's head spins and eyes blacken. The buzzing crowd shouts the countdown. This fight is not going to plan.

Arnold has been practicing boxing ever since he found out about his bully's hobby, refusing to let this acidic slime win. James gets up once more, despite the burning pain he must be feeling. *Crack.*

Arnold blurts out tasteless slang, followed by silent tears. Excruciating, tearing pain. Vile, chilling memories reappear. This was a terrible idea.

Arnold peers into the eyes of his overconfident, twisted rival. Boiling rage engulfs his mind. Arnold releases numbing blows to James' face. James stumbles. *Bam.* James drops hard.

Arnold continues. The crowd hisses. He's going too far. James crawls into a ball, pleading. Bittersweet sensations overshadow the moment. Arnold stops. The crowd is in disgust. Arnold glances at the sticky blood on his hands.

This was not how he had imagined it. Bitter, ugly, regretful revenge.

J. S. Wellian's Biography

Jake Wellian is a 25-year-old Swiss storyteller. Spending his younger years creating stories from his bedroom, Jake sourced inspiration from experiences and his own vivid imagination, solidifying the foundation for his passion for creative writing that he carries today.
www.linkedin.com/in/jake-wellian-41249b134

224: ONE AT A TIME

by Ally Apodochi

They noticed that his hair had changed. Last time they saw it, it was a warm brown, sun-bleached from dark to chocolate. Now it was mint green, possibly faded from a blue dye. It made him look softer in the golden-yellow sunlight peering over their neighbour's fence, threatening to disappear and take away this new pastel version of him.

As they sat on the stoop, they realised he was waiting for a response. They blinked.

"Did you ask me something?"

He sighed. "I asked if you wanted to grab dinner."

They would have scoffed if the sound of his voice didn't lance its way through their heart. It had been a while since they heard the soft musical lilt, and they were almost ready to admit they had missed him. It used to be their most favourite sound in the world.

Used to.

Still, they knew they hadn't eaten all day. On one hand, they'd cave and admit to their feelings. On the other, they'd get to eat. What was there left to lose?

"OK."

Ally Apodochi's Biography

I am a 20-year-old nonbinary English Literature student, striving to write inclusive stories that deal with the emotions many don't like to think about for too long, with themes that are usually influenced by mythology or fantasy.

225: AFTER THE RAIN

by Hajra Saeed

There had been a heavy downpour all morning. By the afternoon, the clouds were gradually dispersing; even the sun had come out. I inhaled the sweet fragrance of the grass, accentuated by the rain.

I took off my shoes and stepped onto the emerald carpet. A tingling feeling shot through me as my feet touched the icy, yet velvety, softness. Closing my eyes, I walked to the end of the garden.

All of a sudden, a sparrow started singing. It was delicately perched on one of the branches of the lemon tree. This was laden with perfectly rounded, bright-yellow fruits and each leaf was studded with translucent pearls. I plucked one and a shower of raindrops fell, unleashing a citrus scent that I could almost taste.

Then, as my gaze shifted upwards, it became momentarily transfixed. For the sun rays were filtering through one of the clouds in such a manner that it literally seemed as if it was an iceberg. A crystallised piece of fluff glittering in the sky...

Hajra Saeed's Biography

Hajra Saeed is a freelance writer in Pakistan, where she has been writing for more than two decades.

226: THAT'S MY DAY SPOILT

by Eileen Baldwin

The train suddenly shrieked to a halt. There was a loud screaming. It was me. I'd been violently thrown forward. My glasses flew off. I felt the roughness of the dirty floor. Then I saw a pair of soft leather shoes. The owner was a young man in a blue suit.

"Are you OK?" He looked worried.

"Yes, thank you," I stammered, and blushed.

By now, I was in my seat. My legs were scratched and purple, my face a deep crimson. I'd been on my way to an interview for a job as a model. Well, that wasn't on the cards anymore.

I wondered if my bright red lipstick was smeared all over my face. I dug my long painted nails into my palms, to stop me laughing hysterically. I looked out of the window and saw primroses.

"Would this make you better?"

I looked up and smelt the flower that my stranger in blue held out to me. The first of many, I hoped.

Eileen Baldwin's Biography

Aged 73, married, three children, four grandchildren. Carer to disabled daughter past 30 years. Published poet in anthologies. Hobbies, crochet and writing. Music, rock and roll, once won a trophy. I have a silly sense of humour.

227: DETERMINED TO PASS

by Khamis Kabeu

Riziki Bidii snapped to attention and listened. "What's that?" she mumbled. *A gun shot*, she thought. For a moment she sat befuddled, trembling with fear.

Just then, a second and third gunshot rent the air. Transfixed, she turned uneasily in her seat, shivering as her stomach spasmed with dread at the roar of gunfire.

Shortly thereafter, more gunshots followed, their rumbling growing closer and closer. She was terror stricken. With the pitch-dark night threateningly still, she felt personally besieged as the combatants continued to advance towards the beleaguered school. Repeatedly, she cocked her head, swivelling it in the direction the sound had come from.

Then, the gunshots stopped and an eerie silence settled over the school and its neighbourhood. And as the silence progressed, it became more and more frightening. She stood up, then sat down, over and over again, the awesome silence conjuring up fearful images of monsters entering the class and tearing her to pieces.

With time, she gathered courage and resumed her studies.

Khamis Kabeu's Biography

I'm an up-and-coming creative writer of the short story and novel. I intend to specialise in the thriller genre, with women as my main characters. I live with my family in Malindi, on the Coast of Kenya.

228: SCENTS AND NO SENSIBILITY

by Gail Everett

Coty's L'Aimant was my mother's favourite perfume when she was a beauty consultant in a London department store. Being a smoker, she travelled to the West End on the uncomfortable and smelly upper deck of the number 11 bus and worked for Beryl, a buyer who was a loud, bossy and conceited woman whose strident voice carried across the entire length of the perfumery.

Whenever I met my mother after work, we ate in Benny's, the nearby wine bar, which offered delicious food, especially their Paddy's Pizza. Doreen, my mother's colleague, would often accompany us, along with the appalling Beryl, and usually got plastered on the house red.

Following one of our outings, Doreen arrived at work the next morning looking like a recently-exhumed corpse, unable to remember the evening in any detail. She touched my mother on the shoulder and asked if the buyer had noticed she was drunk. Mother then had to tell the unfortunate Doreen that everything had been fine, right up to the point when she'd thrown up over Beryl's shoes.

Gail Everett's Biography

Apart from what I told my mother when I was a teenager, my interest in fiction began at the tender age of 63, by which time I had exhausted most other possibilities for pastimes in which to engage whilst sitting down.

229: IN THE SPRING, A YOUNG MAN'S FANCY...

by John Notley

I fell in love with her when, as a 16 year old, I was on a school trip to Paris one spring. We had all been told about her by our young art mistress who was quite a picture herself. I wished that I was alone in the Louvre with her, undisturbed by the chattering and mutterings of those behind me.

I was captivated by the light pallor of her skin, the hands crossed demurely on her lap and the pale throat unadorned with jewellery. If only we could be together, alone. To hold her hands, to touch her breasts, to taste her lips and hear her as she whispered words of love in my ear.

The bell rang indicating closing time and I deliberately remained as the others left, my pubescent eyes gazing into hers, which exuded a sensuality I had never known. An attendant took me by the arm and led me to the exit, still entranced by her beauty.

Art classes were never the same again.

John Notley's Biography

John, a retired travel agent, having nothing better to do, has taken up his pen again and enjoys participating in Chris's challenges. Although the remuneration is nothing to speak of, he has the satisfaction of seeing his work in print.

www.linkedin.com/in/john-notley-503666102/

230: THE MAN IN BLACK

by Kevin J. McLain

The train suddenly lurched forward and Brian was thrown from his seat. He couldn't understand why. The train wasn't going very fast.

As he landed on his knees, he looked around and noticed that there was a man moving very slowly up the aisle towards him. The man was dressed in a black trench coat and a strange blue light was emanating from his body, swirling around him like a slow-moving tornado.

There was a clanging sound – metal food trays bounced against the windows and seats of the cabin as he walked by. Brian got to his feet by pulling himself up, using the rough leather of the seat in front of him.

The man in black held out his hand and blue light shot out in Brian's direction. As it touched him, Brian was lifted off his feet and slammed hard onto the floor of the aisle. There was a bitter-sweet taste of iron in his mouth as he coughed up primrose-coloured blood.

Kevin J. McLain's Biography

Born in Los Angeles, California, and raised in Grants Pass, Oregon. Received his education mostly in the field of computer science, but loves creative writing as well as reading science fiction and fantasy stories.

231: MONDAY MORNING BLUES

by Christine Law

Thinking of Monday morning makes me feel tired. Street light shines through the curtains while the cat purrs. I'm feeling blue, looking at the dark shape of the church. Giving a sigh, I feel like a clown wondering what will make me smile.

Monday, the start of the working week, travelling on the train with the smell of body odour and cigarettes. Occasionally you get the sweet smell of perfume. I try to think pleasant thoughts – primroses, poppies and green fields.

Christine Law's Biography

I enjoy writing. It helps to relieve stress when not working as a live in carer. I have had work in print in *Writers' Forum* magazine, Ian Renee Trust and, recently, letters in local tabloids.

232: BLOOD PRESSURE

by David Silver

He felt a tingling sensation in his wrists. Death was approaching.

Peter admittedly suffered from hypochondria. Actually, he preferred to call it by its longer name, hypochondriasis, because it sounded more serious. But he knew that behind his condition lay an undeniable multitude of fatal illnesses.

By the time he arrived for his begged-for emergency slot at the medical centre, Peter was aware that the bitter taste of anxiety within his clenched jaws meant he was, once again, on borrowed time.

Typically, the doctor didn't seem worried. After conducting a (too cursory) examination, he suggested a blood test at the hospital.

Peter sat bolt upright on the slow-moving bus, seeing the flashing lights and hearing the screaming sirens of the emergency ambulance he *should* have been in.

Stifling a shriek of panic as he saw he was 23rd in the queue inside the hospital's blood room, Peter plucked nervously at his wrists and realised he had removed the elastic bands he always wore as a reminder to take his morning vitamin pills.

David Silver's Biography

David Silver was a reporter, sub-editor and columnist on various newspapers in Greater Manchester, England. He retired in 2002 and from 2011-2016 wrote a column for *The Courier*, a weekly newspaper for UK expatriates in Spain.

www.facebook.com/david.silver.543

233: LATE AGAIN

by Betty Hattersley

It was all go as usual this morning, rushing about, desperately trying to get to work on time. We had an important meeting planned first thing, so it was essential for me to show good grooming and efficiency, as well as good time keeping. Doing my hair and makeup was time consuming, but I didn't want to turn up at the office appearing as if I really had just crawled out of bed.

A strong black coffee would be my breakfast ritual once again this morning. I'd probably grab a sandwich for lunch. But even before leaving my gorgeous apartment, I was already dreaming about returning home this evening to recline on my brand new, soft, leather couch, wrapped in my luscious, soft dressing gown in front of the television, enjoying a well-earned gin and tonic.

Betty Hattersley's Biography

I've had numerous poems and short stories published in anthologies and magazines. I've written verses for greeting cards, had a feature in a calendar and double features in mainstream newspapers. Now I've found a new life on Chris's fantastic website.

234: THE TRAIN WRECK

by Timothy Newnes

The train suddenly nudged from its railway tracks without losing momentum. The engine slowly twisted through 90 degrees, dragging each carriage until all the rolling stock slid sideways. Windows shattered, rough gravel below pulverising and finally ripping through toughened glass, entering the carriages like bullets. The sky was azure blue, a beautiful day. Strange it would be so tragic.

Inside, living and dead bounced off walls, floor and ceiling, gravity drawing them forward to the concertina crush caused by massive deceleration. An alarm, constantly deafening, clanged but was heard by fewer people as each second passed. Breathing, never mind hearing, stopped, brain cells expired. Chairs became missiles, ripping from their bolts, slamming into people obstructing their path.

The detestable man sat on his fold-away chair, spectating from an elevated vantage point beside the railway line culvert. He drank hot, sweet tea, marvelling at his abhorrent creation and that it cost a single dynamite stick. Hundreds would die, or at least he hoped. He paused from appreciating the scene to breathe in summer's primrose fragrance, smiling.

Timothy Newnes' Biography

This is my first challenge submission in the eternal struggle to become a writer, adding to a short story I self-published and a career of writing procurement proposals for the Ministry of Defence that many believe are a work of fiction.

@NewnesTimothy

235: THE BROKEN DOWN TRAIN

by Kenneth Muir

The train suddenly stopped. It was a big surprise to all on board because this was not the end of the journey, or a stopping place along the way.

The man sitting next to me was blue in the face with anxiety as he was scheduled to attend an important meeting that morning: time was of the essence.

Suddenly there was a noise, a clang, coming from the undercarriage of the train. I imagined it had to do with the moving part of the brakes.

After a while, I felt the sudden jerk forward, which was rough to say the least.

I thought about that morning when my mother gave me my breakfast as usual. I enjoyed the sweet milky coffee only she could make.

As I sat on the stationary train, gazing through the window, I rekindled my spirit by watching the primrose plants at the side of the railway tracks. I thought how happy they looked, not having to worry about a broken down train.

Kenneth Muir's Biography

My name is Kenneth Muir, married, British nationality, living in the Philippines since 1987. I chose short story writing as a therapy in my old age. I am 83 years old this year.

236: CARESSING BY THE FIRE

by Claire Apps

Danny smoothly caressed my silky coat, as it hung over my shapely body. Showing my appreciation, I mewed in time with his strokes. The cool wintery weather made itself known as an icy blast hit the windows and rattled the cottage's old oak beams. We were unconcerned about the outside. The log fire blazed away, the heat poured around us.

Just the two of us, lying on the comfy wool rug, gazing into each other's eyes. His were glittering with the sparks of the fire reflecting back, making a surreal moment, like looking into an unearthly being's soul. It startled me. The hair bristling up at the back of my neck, I checked his eyes again. Green eyes – normal, half opened, looking at me. His hand paused, sensing a hesitancy in me. By looking alone, he queried what was wrong. Stretching my long nails outwards, I felt his arm, asking for him to continue the caressing I so longed for.

"You spoil that dog, Danny. Where can I sit to be by the fire?" asked Jane.

Claire Apps' Biography

I have self-published a book of poetry from the soul. I have taught creative writing to vulnerable women, to help them gain self-esteem and confidence, for a number of years.

237: EXIT STRATEGY

by Tony Lawrence

The train suddenly appeared half a mile down the track as I wiped the sweat from my eyes, my heart thumping and reverberating upwards inside my skull. This was my only chance of escaping the blue and red flashing lights of the cop cars all around town, their heavily-armed occupants intent on my capture.

I heard the bell clang as the train slowed across the viaduct and the freight cars bumped and jostled each other in response. My shaking hands clutched the rough canvas bag containing the stolen cash and I breathed deeply to steady myself. My mouth was parched, the sweet minty taste of gum long gone.

I'd hidden at the meadow's edge, the smell of wild primroses recalling my childhood games on the farm. Now, I crouched in readiness. Let the engine go past, count 10 cars, run alongside, grab the steel ladder and pull myself aboard. Easy in the movies, but I'm carrying 200,000 dollars and still wearing my pencil skirt and high heels. "Time to go," I said.

Tony Lawrence's Biography

Writing as Tony Lawrence, I am a recently retired businessman living in North Yorkshire with my wife, two cats, drum kit and plenty of time to practice my writing hobby.

238: THE UNEXPECTED

by Aashana Daru

My heart is aching. The smell of gunpowder in the air is overpowering, I can almost taste it. The rustling of the leaves surrounding me is more deafening than the bullets piercing the air. I turn my head and see Jack sink like a heap of bones – bullet to the chest. My eyes fill up and I have to choke back a cough, or puke, I'm not sure which.

Amidst the pain and suffering, the sunlight falls softly on the forest floor, illuminating the spatters of blood and fallen bodies. And then, suddenly, all gunfire ceases. No leaf rustles. And then I hear it: the typical whir of an airline engine.

I steel myself, a tear trickling down my grimy cheek. My heartbeat echoes in my ears as I hold my breath, waiting for the bomb to drop, almost expecting the blast. I mutter a prayer as I hear the chamber latch open, the missile dropping, but suddenly...

"Sweetheart, dinner's ready."

The book falls out of my hands.

Aashana Daru's Biography

Aashana loves writing plot twists. And descriptions. And stories. Pretty much everything; she just loves writing. The only thing that she loves more than writing is reading. With her newfound love for war literature, she's always up for book recommendations.

239: UNREAL DISBELIEF

by Alice Hale

You feel sad.

The tears burn your eyes, pricking their corners like tiny knives or barbed wire.

A hazy mist covers your vision. All that is left is colour, there are no more clear shapes.

The scents of salty tears and dark chocolate dance through the air in a waltz of grief. You can still taste the remnants of the delicacy on your tongue. Not unlike your current mental state, it is bitter.

The background noise continues.

When you finally awaken from your daze, the screen is black.

It's over.

You can't believe they killed your favourite character.

Alice Hale's Biography

Alice is a 17-year-old hobbyist writer from the Netherlands. She only started writing a couple of months ago. Her hobbies include reading, writing, listening to music and making bad jokes.

240: GRANDMA'S SECRET

by Joyce Bingham

Grandma adored the conservatory. In summer, she basked in the intense heat, wearing her clip on sunglasses, so she could read her book or watch the voraciously noisy magpies in the garden. It was excellent for her arthritis, she exclaimed. "It takes away some of the pain and I can smell the headiness of the roses from the garden." It also helped to have a gin and tonic and a ginger biscuit to delight the tongue, so she said.

When we brought her ashes home in the polished wood casket, it only seemed fitting that she rested in the conservatory. We all caressed the smooth wood and muttered our thoughts to her. She started haunting us with love, the overwhelming scent of her lavender perfume filling the conservatory. The children would scream in delight, "We can smell Grandma." It brought her back to us, kept her close, helped us grieve.

During a thorough spring clean, I found the old lavender room freshener hidden in the conservatory behind Grandma's chair. I put it back.

Joyce Bingham's Biography

Joyce has been writing scientific English for too many years. She has rekindled her original love of fiction writing. In the planning stages of a novel, she has embraced flash fiction to sharpen her mind on plotting and editing.

241: MELANCHOLIA

by Maria V A Johnson

Darkness:
Shadows abound in shades of grey,
all colour leeched from the surroundings.
Temperature plummets; ice freezes to my heart.
Rain falls torrential; a barrier to deaden my senses.
Wind ravages; roaring through my mind.
A mirror: the stranger stands tall and calm;
laughs and jokes, always upbeat.
I scream in silence; unseen behind the reflection,
I drown in a sea of despair.
Heaviness drags me to the ground.
I struggle to raise my head;
fight the pull of gravity.
I try to see through the darkness,
but there's no hope in sight.

Dawning:
The sun bursts through the clouds,
chases the shadows away, but only on the surface.
The darkness within my heart,
rises and falls like the tide, lacking regularity;
often spurred on by outside influences.
Temperature rises, warms my skin;
my heart still a frozen block, unmelted.
A gentle breeze, no tumult in my mind,
brushes my body, awakens my senses; but only a little.
The stranger's light happiness,
reflected by the mirror,
penetrates through my outer shell.
Gravity loses its hold, I raise my head.

Hope shines weakly in the distance.

Light:
The clouds part, burnt away;
the midday sun removes all shadows.
Equatorial heat burns through to my heart.
A rain of blossoms soothes my senses;
alive and vibrant with the onset of spring.
The thick, uncomfortable blanket of emotion,
pent up throughout my life,
that once smothered and buried me,
has turned to insubstantial air.
The mirror shatters around me;
no longer a stranger, I stand tall and calm,
as I step through the crumbling frame.
I am surrounded by hope,
as I confidently stride into the future.

Maria V A Johnson's Biography

Maria V A Johnson is a voracious reader, professional editor, and published author and poet with a Bachelor of Arts Honours Degree in English and Creative Writing.
www.maria7627.wordpress.com

242: UNFAIR

by Cathy Cade

Competing hurdy-gurdy sounds call from the bus stop. Your foot sinks in slippery mud and you almost fall. Tonight's dry weather is a good omen on this last day of the funfair.

Candyfloss is a childish indulgence, its fluffy sweetness dissolving as you fold portions into your mouth. Hot doughnuts tempt you, but you walk on until the burnt sugar smell gives way to fried onions. Time for all that later, when you're shivering bone-deep, waiting for him to finish work.

Through moving bodies and flashing colours, amid the cacophony of music, screams, laughter, dinging bells and, "Roll up, roll up," you spot him negotiating dodgem cars to join a girl at the edge. The ride's music gets louder and cars begin to move.

Her hand is in his.

You remember its warmth last night, holding yours.

They kiss.

He surfaces to meet your damp gaze. An eyebrow lifts, a shoulder shrugs and that heart-stopping smile is confident of forgiveness.

And you would, indeed, forgive. If only you knew where to find him next.

Cathy Cade's Biography

Cathy, a retired librarian, swapped Dewey decimals for competition wordcounts and has had stories published in *Scribble*, *Flash Fiction Magazine* and three anthologies (most notably, *To Hull And Back Short Story Anthology 2018*).

www.cathy-cade.com

243: FROM THE PARK BENCH

by Jayne Morgan

As she sat down on the park bench, a menagerie of smells titillated Nicola's nostrils. Fresh, salient, newly cut grass; sweet, fragrant roses; the rich tantalising smell of someone's coffee.

In the distance, children were playing. She heard their gleeful squeals of delight; cheerful giggles of exuberance and their dismissive grumbles of unfairness as they bickered with their siblings.

She reached inside her bag and pulled out the small chocolate bar. The paper rustled like leaves in the breeze as she unwrapped it. She broke a piece off and heard it snap like the crack of a whip. She put the broken piece into her mouth and let its smooth, sweet taste melt on her tongue.

Nicola welcomed the soothing embrace of the breeze as it caressed her bare arms. Beside her feet, Casey, her dog, brushed up against her legs. She reached down to pet him and felt the warmth of his fur and the cold metal of his harness. Nicola couldn't see a thing, but she could visualise everything.

Jayne Morgan's Biography

My book *Haunted School* was published in 2005 as part of Hodder's Livewire series. Since then, I have written two more (as yet unpublished) books. When I'm not writing, I work as a support assistant to students with learning difficulties.

244: BLUE PERSUASION

by David Michael Inverso

Blue-green shimmered from far down the dimly lit corridor. Quickly, it resolved into distinctly feminine hips swaying, bare shoulders tilting, the outline of a thigh brightening with each forward step and then vanishing into twinkling aquamarine folds of cloth. An oval face with large dark eyes came into focus. Penelope.

AJ smiled appreciatively. Penelope's outfit hugged her hips and thighs, flaring wide from mid-calf to the floor. Glimmering, lagoon blue cloth swept up over her chest to loop around her neck. Her long, dark hair was set into a braid that arced over her head backward from her forehead. Tiny sea-blue lights twinkled in the braid.

She smiled brightly with glistening turquoise lipstick on lips perfectly shaped for kissing. Pearl white teeth flashed as she said, "You sweet man, coming to meet me. This area is so—" Her brown eyes grew bigger as she glanced around. Her smile faltered for a moment. "So unusual."

She planted a feathery kiss on his cheek, just long enough and wet enough to curl his toes.

David Michael Inverso's Biography

David Michael Inverso, from Seattle, writes sci-fi, fantasy and horror. He's had published exactly half a short story in the inaugural edition of *Unction* magazine. It never published again. And in October 2019, 'Mulch' in *Rune Bear Weekly*.

245: MIRACLES CAN HAPPEN

by Alan Barker

I heard the door creak open, then footsteps as someone entered, shoes squeaking.

Little Rosie began sobbing. I pulled her closer; her whole body was shaking.

Now I heard him ambling round the classroom, tapping each desk, breathing hoarsely.

"You're here somewhere," he chirped. "I'm gonna wheedle you out and when I do—"

A volley of gunshots crashed over our heads, tearing into the blackboard. The pungent smell of nitroglycerine filled the air, leaving my throat dry as dust.

An eerie silence followed. Had he cottoned on to our hiding place? Silently, I prayed for a miracle.

Steps approached. Finally, he appeared, peering under the desk and grinning.

I clambered to my feet and said, "Hey, dude. Good game, huh?"

Rosie screamed.

I hit the deck just before the shots rang out. Behind me came the sounds of glass breaking and crashing.

I looked up. The screwball was lying motionless, blood seeping from his mouth. In the doorway stood a police officer, rifle in hand.

My prayer for a miracle had been answered.

Alan Barker's Biography

Alan, a retired tax accountant, lives within a horse's gallop of Epsom Racecourse and is a season ticket holder at Woking FC (sadly). He enjoys writing daft stories which occasionally get published when he cuts out the silly speling misteaks.

246: FINALLY, MORNING

by Carla Vlad

I couldn't shake the feeling that I was floating in a really cold, still body of water.

The world around me was completely silent. I tried to listen for any noise, but there was nothing. My room was swallowed by the darkness. There was no shadow. No light.

I tried to breathe, but I couldn't. I wanted to move, but I was afraid I'd drown. I started hearing this terrifying noise and I realised that I was screaming. I stopped so I could breathe again.

Slowly, I realised the cold water around me felt like my bedsheets. My eyes got used to the darkness. I could see the furniture in my room. Second by second, I felt safer and safer.

I tried to move again. I started with my legs, then my arms and, in the end, I ran to turn on the light. I checked the time. Finally, morning.

Carla Vlad's Biography

Carla is a creative writing student with a huge passion for people and art. She is always looking for the next opportunity to learn. Someone told her she could win a Pulitzer and that is all she can think about.

247: SENSING DANGER

by Isabel Flynn

The train suddenly lurched forward and back, then screeched to a halt. We peered out the window with a look of surprise. Armed men in black hoods rushed past.

We ducked down shaking and I whispered to the elderly, blue-haired lady next to me, "Are we safe?" I knew the answer by her enormous eyes and trembles.

We smelt smoke and it tasted acrid on our tongues. A bell clanged, but nothing was visible. We were only about five miles from the next station. Someone must realise we had stopped.

The floor felt rough and dirty, and a sour milk carton squished against my nose, making me sneeze. I pushed it away and the same lady growled, "Careful." I felt annoyed. She wasn't as sweet as I thought.

Gosh, I was filthy and would be late for work. Presentation was the main thing at the posh Primrose Hotel where I worked. Of course, I had to survive first.

That's when we heard the driver announce, "Just safety practice, back in your seats, we're off again."

Isabel Flynn's Biography

A born-again writer after 30 years absence, when work, children, and more work interposed. Doing some courses so the words flow in the best possible way. Loving it.

www.thefamilytapestry.blogspot.com

248: PRE-LOVED

by Kathryn Joyce

Although the mustiness of abandoned apparel tickles her nose, Ginny loves charity shops. But this perfumery of a 'pre-loved' emporium is akin to sneaking chocolate on a diet – irresistible.

A cloud of yolk-yellow sweater caresses her hand. It's almost... She knows its loose knit will catch the draught and will reveal her underwear. It's a size too big, and the price is seven times that of a charity shop sweater.

Surreptitiously, she googles the label, sees a similar jumper in red. Finest Merino. *£149.*

£30 pounds suddenly seems reasonable. And oversized sweaters are so forgiving.

Kathryn Joyce's Biography

Kathryn Joyce's debut novel, *Thicker Than Soup*, was published in 2015. Short stories have appeared in anthologies including *Stories in Colour*, *Borderline Stories*, and *To Hull And Back*. Kathryn says she enjoys writing about the vagaries of life.

249: THE MEANING OF LIFE

by Fatemeh Momeni

We have come to see suffering,
To help people,
Let us be upset, smile.
We have come to make, see and hear,
Learn from those who are sitting and not trying.
Let us rise and shout love,
We love each other.
The meaning of life is the meaning of human existence.
What is meant by man?
Man means pain and pleasure,
Efforts and hardships.
Women of the community,
Start flying to your dreams.
This life gives you strength.
Men of the community, be strong, be strong,
Stay with the women so they can rely on your steady mountain to reach their peak of pleasure and desire.
Fight for your dreams.
The meaning of life is to live.
It's a little harder to look at life.
Look at easy life.
We didn't come to eat and sleep,
And embrace being alone,
Be on the fly,
On the horizon of happiness,
How the aortic pain passed.
Was it easy or hard?
Not being or being?
This is important, but makes us happy about being and going.

Fatemeh Momeni's Biography

I'm Fatemeh Momeni, 18 years old, from Iran. I went through a life full of pain and hardship. In the midst of all the hardships, I learned hope. I took the pen and wrote everything that came to my mind.

250: PRESENCE

by Jacek Wilkos

I'm lying on the beach. The July sun disappeared behind the horizon a while ago. There is no soul in sight, only nature surrounds me, untouched by human hands. Memories come back alive.

The sea whispers your name, the wind strokes my face with your kisses, still, warm sand reminds me of your cuddled body and the stars shine with the glow of your eyes. It almost feels like you're here with me. I fall asleep with a smile.

But at some moment the wind will stop, the sea will calm, the sand will cool and the stars will hide behind the clouds. The next day, when the sun rises and the sunlight wakes me up, I will still be alone. At the beach and in my life.

Jacek Wilkos' Biography

Jacek Wilkos is an engineer from Poland. He lives with his wife and daughter in the beautiful city of Cracow. He is addicted to buying books and loves coffee, dark ambient music and riding his bike.

www.facebook.com/Jacek.W.Wilkos/

251: THAT DAY

by Jasmine Lee

"It was raining that day. I could see grey clouds for miles and everything looked darker around me but so much clearer. The rain was coming down pretty heavily and I remember feeling all of the raindrops hit me as my jacket became slowly soaked more and more. In the background, I could hear the sounds of thunder rolling in. Judging by the weather, I knew it would be a great weekend." I leaned back against the hard grey chair, shivering. Feeling the cold metal against my back, I jumped, sitting up straight.

"So it sounds like you were in a good mood. What made you change? Why did you do what you did?" The therapist stared, waiting for an answer.

"Well..." I started.

The door banged open and the room became ten times colder as a man walked in. His pungent cologne stank, spreading throughout the room. He flashed his badge before sitting down.

I was then reminded once again that I was trapped in an interrogation room, replaying my story.

Jasmine Lee's Biography

Jasmine likes to occasionally write short stories and little scenes. She also had a much harder time writing her short biography than writing the actual story (and after much deliberation has been able to come up with two subpar sentences).

252: THE INTRUDER

by Matilda Pinto

In a gallery classroom, deep and dark, stood a frail lady, delivering lines from Macbeth.

"Welcome to act one, scene one," she thundered, walking zigzag, whizzing up and down the dais and thumping on the table, dum, dum, dum...

And then, they heard a strange hiss.

The class sat on the edge of their seats, not knowing what to expect.

Next, in a blood curdling voice, the lady simulated the witches all, the storm, thunder and lightning too. From her flowed a diabolic rhythm, rising and falling, "Fair is foul, and foul is fair." Thereafter, "Meet Macbeth the macabre," she rumbled, only to be interrupted by a series of hisses.

Had Paddock entered the scene before its call?

Ding dong, dong, rang the bell. As chased by the witches, the class spilled out of the door.

Alone and still, she stood and heard the hisses, yet again.

Did the lady spot the hooded creature, slithering out from under the very dais where she stood, in no hurry whatsoever? He wasn't part of the cast, was he?

Matilda Pinto's Biography

Matilda was once complimented for her role as a witch. We have as much of the wicked in us as the virtuous, she beamed. We become what we choose to be. She has penned a novel and a few short stories.
www.facebook.com/matilda.pinto.9

253: A BLAST FROM THE PAST

by Alexandra Klyueva

The same old house.

The same rusty door.

I remember my childhood.

I step carefully on the rotten boards. They make the same creaking sound with every step. As a child, I was afraid of this sound. But today I am glad to hear it.

I go into the room. I take a deep breath and remember the sweet smell of my mother's perfume. It was my favourite smell. Now all I can smell is rust and dust. It tickles my nose and I pinch it with my fingers.

I run my hand over the old, rough table. Every crack in it is a story of my childhood and my hobbies.

I walk over the shards that get stuck in my shoes. The mirror on the wall is broken. I carefully take a shard and point it toward the sun. A ray of sunlight comes rushing into the room, and its thin path illuminates a black chest in the corner of the room.

What is it?

Alexandra Klyueva's Biography

My name is Alexandra Klyueva, I'm 20 and I live in Russia. Every story I write is a desire to turn my thoughts into letters and share it with people.

254: HEAVEN'S ROWBOAT

by Quilly Epithet

A thousand silver stars reflected themselves in the sea, with water so unnaturally still waves dared not disturb the constellations and bright blues of the skies above. The rowboat creaked as it moved.

The oars dripped as the woman rowed forward through the night. Her hands aching, moving rhythmically as if rowing through the sky. Beneath the layers of blankets her child stirred. She held his small body close to her, feeling his warmth despite the wetness of the boat. A tang of salt on her dry lips.

If this was the end of her and the baby, at least they had made it to Heaven.

Quilly Epithet's Biography

Quilly Epithet has been ghost-writing stories for three and a half years. She lives in Australia with her cat Alexander.

@QuillyEpithet

255: TINNITUS TAMED

by Alan D. Przybylski

Waves crashing against rocks, fingernails screeching against blackboards, along with varied pops, crackles and whistles. All of this against the backdrop of a constant, high-pitched whine. These are just a few of the worst noises I hear every second of every day since I can remember.

Horrified? Wait, I haven't finished the half of it yet. The volume, you could not imagine. Like a siren blasting two metres from my face, it is relentless. Tossing restless nights away, sweat-soaked sheets tying me in knots. This causes my thin-necked, worn vertebrae to trap nerves and waves of savage pain wash across the back of my neck. I feel sick at these times, dizzy, sometimes for days, like a permanent migraine. Coloured lightning flashes across my vision, burning its message into my brain. Senses all heighten, especially smell. The slightest whiff of food sets me running for the bathroom.

After 64 years, I have finally found the cure. The bus driver didn't have a chance to brake.

Alan D. Przybylski's Biography

A 64 year old cockney geezah (born within the sounds of Bow Bells), I moved to Brentwood in Essex to raise a family at the age of 19. Telecommunications were my trade for over 30 years.

256: THE CASTLE

by Kelly Yeung

The rusty metal door creaked open all by itself, revealing the seemingly endless darkness within.

I stepped into the castle, my footsteps echoing in the eerie silence. The eyes of the painted people on the wall seemed to follow me as I ventured in further, causing the hairs on the back of my neck to rise.

Crunch.

I jumped, stifling a scream as I realised I'd stepped on a ghostly white bone. I backed into a wall, only to touch something sticky: spider webs.

I turned to flee back through the door, but it clanged shut the moment the thought entered my mind. There was nowhere to go but up the spindly stairs.

I placed my hand on the banisters, but shrank back immediately. It was covered in goo, and I caught a whiff of something metallic.

The pale moon shone through the pane-less windows, and my mouth became dry at what I saw. The dead body lying there, a pool of blood oozing onto the tiled floor.

Kelly Yeung's Biography

Kelly is an aspiring writer studying in Hong Kong. She loves painting, acting, singing, and reads every day.

257: THE KNEELING GENERATION

by Justin Payne

"Why would I do that?" asked Angie in angst, desperately scanning the vast English sheep hills on the crisp afternoon from their peak in elevation at the side of the road. He was in another one of his tantrums, shouting into her ear from above.

"For one thing, because I have a gun pointed at your head and we are a couple of kilometers from the nearest witness. I'm a professional, Angie. So tell me where it is, or I'll take what's left in our joint bank account as compensation."

Angie began to sob, her eyes growing soggy like the knees of her jeans in the cold grass. She tasted the cod on his breath. No wonder they didn't go to lunch. She usually pitied her brother during these outbursts, but now she feared his cold barrel digging into her temple.

She couldn't believe the relief she felt saying it, betraying herself forever. Her words cut through her lips like they cut through the idling sedan's oppressive exhaust. "I hid your passport in the trunk sleeve."

Justin Payne's Biography

Mr Payne was technically a published author at age 12 for a school poem comparing controlling your life in opposition to the controls for a VHS player. Now a web developer, he is returning to writing as an unpublished novelist.

258: MONDAY, MONDAY, CAN'T TRUST THAT DAY

by Roger Newton

Mondays often make me nervous. I arrive at work early, trying to remember what I'm doing. It's easy if I'm travelling overseas because other things remind me that I'm not going into the office today. Early morning journeys to Manchester Airport across the Pennines, enhanced particularly by blue sky, would usually set my mind at ease.

This is not one of those days. In the fitting shop, a loud clang greets me. Someone is knocking seven bells out of a metal hinge.

"Wrong drawing, boss. No time to make another. By bending the hinge we can make the cover fit. Then we shall bring in our cosmetic department. They'll do something for the rough surface we've created."

"That work needs Vic Faulkner's rubber stamp on it, Peter, so give him a sweet smile. Remember, no Lloyds' signature on the shipping documents..."

"No delivery to Hull. Ask him if his primrose came first at the flower show, boss. He was confident that its scent alone would steal the red rosette."

"I'd forgotten about that. Thanks, Peter."

Roger Newton's Biography

Writing is something I love doing. In particular, I enjoy passing on a story using as few words as possible. There are such things as fate and coincidence and other occurrences that defy the imagination. I've plenty to write about.

259: BACK IN BUSINESS

by Ashutosh Pant

I still remember how yummy the meals were, how the fragrance made my full tummy hungry. Alas, all that has gone. How many people lost their jobs? I feel sorry for them.

I talked to the owner and, after lots of negotiations, we agreed to restart the business. Now, I'm happy seeing people back at work. I am proud hearing the sound of the old trailer moving and smelling the delicious aromas. The mobile restaurant was back.

Ashutosh Pant's Biography

My name is Ashutosh Pant. I study in class 7. I am 13 years old.

260: MANGO DELIGHT

by Majella Pinto

Every monsoon break, the two boys visit their grandma, never once forgetting to raid her freezer to bring out the crackling bag of frozen Hafoos mangoes, saved just for them because they live in lands bereft of mango groves.

They're excited to see Grandma, surfacing from the icy vapors of the freezer with plump mangoes. She peels them, removing their streaked and shrivelled skin, otherwise endowed with a vibrant cadmium orange hue. The impatient boys salivate as she slices them into juicy chunks.

With the tasty sweetness oozing from their mouths, Grandma gets busy wiping the juicy glaze from their sticky faces. The chewy pith is left for the finale.

With their tiny fingers digging deep into the pith for a firm grip, they go for it, cheeks, chin and nose lunging for the succulent bites, leaving a golden mess running through their fingers, down their elbows, drip, drip, drip.

Finally, with grateful belly burps, the boys say, "Dev Borem Korum (God bless you)," and run off into the woods to chase the monkeys.

Majella Pinto's Biography

Majella Pinto, raised in India, is an artist and writer based in California. She works in Silicon Valley and is devoutly focused on her twin passions of art and literature.

www.facebook.com/majella.pinto

261: OUR LADY OF THE STAIRS

by John Di Carlo

Stairwells were dark in the 1960s; at least where I grew up. Black as pitch by night and grey as an ancient headstone by day.

Descend them in summer and you plunged into a disused well: chill air clung to warm skin, dank with the brackish taste of sweat. Climb them in winter and you slipped on ice; crystals that gathered like school bullies, tripping you to the ground.

Every tenant had to clean the stairs: written in your tenancy, black and white. Except they didn't. Old May cleaned the stairs. For 2s 6d she knelt on thick knees, big hands red and raw, oozing the tang of Dettol, scrubbing every step. That's where they found her, sprawled by her bucket, dead from a heart attack.

Our lady of the stairs, my father called her. He spoke at her funeral. His voice rang through the empty church like a giant bell. Whenever I see stone stairwells, I see Old May – on her knees, scrubbing – our lady of the stairs.

John Di Carlo's Biography

I started writing at age 8 and won my first prize at age 10 from the RSPCA. I stopped writing at 17 after listening to sensible people. I resumed at 65 when I stopped being sensible.

262: THE FIVE SENSES AND THEIR DOWNFALLS

by Rose Bingley

Have you ever felt the heat of the sun touch the very back of your neck? That warm, beautiful, balmy feeling that ends in a red irritation of the skin.

Have you ever smelled the crisp smell of the Cheeto? That cheesy, tasteful tang that ends in an overindulgence and fattening of the body.

Have you ever tasted a dessert? Of course you have, and that's why you are pudgy.

Have you ever seen the daisy in the field, that beautiful white and yellow thing open its arm and bloom? I haven't seen anything.

Rose Bingley's Biography

My name is Rose Bingley and I have written since I was six and read since way before that. I live in the PNW with my family.

263: TRANSITION

by Maryam Hodaee

Thrown down, I looked up and saw a high cement ceiling with the tallest grey crooked walls and countless rooms around it. I could smell the dampness from every corner. The only sounds were cringy little rattles from everywhere and my heavy breathing echoing in the mysterious angles. *Insects, my worst fear.*

I could feel coldness coming off the walls, giving me goose bumps on my naked arms. I'd been staring at an imaginary dot in shock for so long that my eyes started to water. Sensing my tears' wetness rolling down my cheeks – followed instantly by feeling little legs moving up my toes – shocked my brain so hard that I jumped half a metre up in my bed as I came back to reality. I sighed with relief. "Thank God it was a dream."

Getting comfortable in my new-found serenity, I could taste the sweetness of being horror-free when I suddenly heard a cringy rattle sound close to my ear. Now I smell lavender. It's nice in here. They call it Heaven.

Maryam Hodaee's Biography

My name is Maryam Hodaee. I'm 32 and Persian. I studied English literature. I am a painter and a lyricist. This is my first time writing a story. I have written poetry, humour and movie scripts.

264: THE UNPUBLISHED BOOK

by Peggy Gerber

"Why would I ever agree to that?"

I'd just received my 25th rejection letter and my husband Charlie was still encouraging me to send my book to more publishers. Couldn't he tell I felt as blue as a festering bruise?

I said, "Charlie, I'm taking every last denial and burying it in the backyard with all my hopes and dreams."

Just then, Charlie dropped a pot on the floor and the clang startled me out of my pity party. As I looked up, I noticed Charlie was holding something behind his back.

I yelled, "I can't take another rejection, it's too rough on me. And what you are hiding?"

Charlie put his arms around me and said, "I think your book is wonderful. I'm certain some publisher will offer you a deal as sweet as honey."

Charlie then pulled out an acceptance letter from Primrose Publishing. He had secretly sent out my manuscript and they loved it.

I never thought I would be so happy to have a sneaky, lying husband.

Peggy Gerber's Biography

Peggy began writing when she became an empty nester. She has been published in *Potato Soup Journal*, *Daily Science Fiction*, *Spillwords* and others. She thanks Chris Fielden for his writing course and supplying the random words that inspired this story.

265: JOURNEY TO A BLUE FRONT DOOR

by Phil Hatchard

The train suddenly jumped.

The trees outside turned from green to yellow. Peter's chest tightened. What would he find had changed at home? Would his front door be blue? Would the flowers smell less like old socks? Would his wife be there?

He hadn't seen her in six months. Lost to another existence so long, he wondered if she'd be the same. She used to love tickle fights. Would she still? They gave Peter stomach cramps but he'd welcome one now. The last six months had been rough.

The train was faster now, he noticed. There seemed to be fewer stations. The seats felt smoother. Cleaner.

The lady opposite offered him a sweet to suck on.

"Helps with the nausea."

He'd heard this before but he never found it helped.

"I'm Primrose," she said. "Or, I used to be." Her voice crackled like part of her was once lost across the boundary but she'd somehow held on.

Still holding the sweet out to Peter. He took it. It tasted worse than before.

Phil Hatchard's Biography

Phil is a doodler, a scribbler and a teacher of maths. He enjoys puns and dancing and has dabbled in acting and stand-up comedy. He once helped set up a charity in his friend's village in Tanzania.
  @evilflea

266: LET THE WORLD COME TO YOU

by Joe Brothers

Sit with a cup of tea and let the world come to you.
And you do.
And it does.

You close your eyes and breathe in deep, enjoying this little ritual of yours. The heat of the teacup prickles your palms as you bring it close to your face. The bitter, earthy tones, the floral notes jutting through like weeds through concrete – a welcome intrusion of the natural world.

That smell takes you by the hand and leads you out into the garden, the tea's aroma only a prelude. The smell of rain-kissed dirt comes to you, the cacophony of flowers jostling for attention, like an orchestra tuning up.

Birdsong cuts through, the coos and caws as well, accompanied by the ever-present susurrus of wind rustling the leaves. That wind ruffles your hair, kisses your cheeks, brings the smells ever closer.

The gentle touch of something landing on your finger startles you, a butterfly or ladybird, but you daren't open your eyes to find out for fear of spooking it and breaking the spell.

Joe Brothers' Biography

Joe Brothers, like director Danny Boyle, studied at Bangor University. Joe, too, works in the film industry – as a barista in a cinema's coffee shop. When not spelling people's names wrong on cups, Joe can be found enthusiastically writing.

267: JUST A SANDWICH'S WORTH

by Kathryn J Barrow

Winds rustled trees. A slight breeze danced in her hair. I soaked up the scent of sweet, strawberry shampoo and vanilla musk. The sun caught it, creating a rainbow of gold that leprechauns would have killed for. I was mesmerised.

I pulled my eyes away and looked upon the blanket. Only one sandwich left. Soon, we'd be done.

She picked it up and halved it, handing me my share. Words seemed vacant, like silence was our aphrodisiac. The touch of her finger over mine, as she placed it in my hand, sent shivers down my spine.

I took a bite. Flavours of cheese and pickle danced on my tongue with sweet delight, before the acidic vinegar settled, curbing my appetite.

I didn't want it to end. I wanted to immerse myself in this happy place. I begged for it as I helped her pack up.

Then we hit the footpath, heard the cars, smelled the fumes and watched people hurry past. All the happy ebbed away and was lost forever.

Kathryn J Barrow's Biography

Kathryn grew up in a small village, left home at 16 and built a career in retail. Then, at 29, she found the confidence to study part-time completing an open degree, concentrating in design and creative writing.

268: AFTER THE STORM

by Vivian Leung

The nights there were usually calm and beautiful: the gentle glow of the moon, the sparkling light of the stars, the soft lulling of the ocean waves. But not that night. That night, there was a fearsome storm. The thunder roared and the lightning cracked. The wind howled and the sky seemed to shed a thousand tears. The villagers who lived near the coast were able to escape but the same could not be said of their coastal homes and possessions. The menacing hands of the ocean waves destroyed all in its path without mercy.

The following morning, all that was left were fragments: fragments of the pots that once made delicious stews, fragments of the picture frames that once held precious memories, fragments of what used to be homes. But amidst all of the destruction, a ray of light fell from the sky and spotlighted a small, pink conch shell glistening on the beach – a gift of the ocean and a reminder that even with all the destruction, the world can still be beautiful.

Vivian Leung's Biography

Although one of her goals in life is to land a career in healthcare, Vivian Leung has always held a love for music and writing. There are few things that are more rewarding to her than helping others.

269: THE DRIFTER

by Joseph Mould

I was always thought a drifter, restlessly unable to settle. A blast of fresh, cool, salt-laden ocean spray reminds me of this as the wind hurls itself into the sails above me, the canvas cracking violently in reply.

The wooden hull of my sailboat creaks with tangible agony under the assault of the waves, which stretch out unforgivingly as far as the eye can see. The tumultuous and foaming mouth of the ocean gapes, ready to consume my little sailboat and its unlikely captain.

I wake suddenly to the smash of glass, as the empty vodka bottle retreats from the grip of my numbed fingers. Consciousness returning, I feel my icy, cold feet as I stretch deeply into my cheap, itchy, damp sleeping bag. The harsh stone step beneath me is as cold, hard and unforgiving as life.

This morning somehow feels different though; my alcohol numbed mind stirs and finally registers the brightly-coloured knitted blanket resting on top of me as, for the first time, I feel the warmth of human kindness.

Joseph Mould's Biography

My name is Joe Mould. I'm 34 years young and live in North Lincolnshire. I am a new writer with bags of enthusiasm. I'm still working on the talent part.

270: THE SCENT OF MOONLIGHT

by Barbara Eustace

Night falls, and I look out into the back garden on this midsummer night, taking in all the familiar scenes. The pale green of the leaves on the apple tree as they turn to grey, the mud-brown of the pond as it darkens to black.

I wait for her and suddenly, there she is, silver shimmering off the leaves, her reflection in the pond. I feel the pain of my longing for her as I get ready for her embrace.

I reach down. The titian hair on my legs is coarse to the touch and I notice it is spreading on my arms, my hands. More pain as tendons rearrange themselves, bones realign.

And then I am hers. She sings to me in her silvery voice, promising satisfaction as the scent of the earth reaches my nostrils. I will prowl this night, I will run barefoot through the forest, I will hunt until I can taste flesh and blood on my tongue. Only then will I be satisfied.

Barbara Eustace's Biography

A lady of leisure since retiring in 2018, I now have plenty of time for writing in my copious spare time. Like a challenge to see where my brain takes me.

271: MIDDAY SUN

by Glo Curl

Sweat trickles down my back, my thighs are burning and my head feels like cotton wool. Looking skyward, I see vapour trails – the first for a long time – and I follow the flight path until my eyes ache from squinting.

I take a large swig of orange juice, cool and sharply sweet, as a gentle breeze carries the scent of the white buddleia to my nostrils; festooned with bees and butterflies gorging on its sticky nectar, it fills the corner of my small garden. The heat is too powerful for the birds. They are sheltering quietly in the trees and bushes, but the steady thrumming of a tractor baling the meadow's midsummer cut drifts into earshot.

Suddenly feeling excruciatingly hot, I stumble from my chair onto the cool welcoming grass and the dog ambles over to join me, licking my salty arms before flopping down again in the shade.

This dog is not mad, but maybe I am.

Glo Curl's Biography

Glo dabbles in poetry and flash fiction, enjoying the discipline of brevity; moreover, she's lazy and anything longer than 500 words would be a chore.

272: AN OBLIGATORY DUTY

by Shawn Maher

Arising from bed, he swiped a hand across his back as a bead of sweat drizzled down like a tiny insect scurrying for a meal. Lumbering to the window, he gazed upon the vast field of green, soaked in sunlight. Sliding into pants, he determined that a shirt was unnecessary for his task. After the impression of a grainy granola bar on his dry palate, and a bitter, black coffee washing it down, he dreaded what he had to do.

From his workshop, he pushed out the mighty metal machine. Clenching a small handle tightly, he tore backwards with extraordinary force. *CHA-CHUNK.* Then silence. His face went redder from the intense heat and his eyes scanned the perimeter. Nobody around. Owing to a second try, the machine let out a continuous buzz. Now everyone would know his affairs.

Guiding the machine across the field, he was overcome with the most agreeable fragrance associated with torment; the agony of grass which was being sheared. Having accomplished his objective, he promptly returned home.

Shawn Maher's Biography

Shawn Maher is a teacher, researcher, musician and amateur writer from Dutchess County, NY. He lives with his awesome wife and two cats. His writing consists of real-world experiences that are not always his own. This one is.

273: LILIES FOR LILY

by R.R. Young

I always wanted my mother to wear makeup. She never did, preferring a more natural appearance.

Leaving by the stage door for the last time, I knew why.

At the florists, I bought her ten hybrid lilies.

"Would you like them gift wrapped?" asked the girl with blue eyelids.

"Just as they are, thank you. You see, they're for someone with strong views and emotions. She believes that natural scent, colour and form in life can't be improved artificially."

R.R. Young's Biography

I'm retired. My interests are jazz piano, dancing, gardening, painting and creative writing. Five short online courses with ICE at Madingley College, Cambridge, has opened a new world. I love it, especially the people from around the globe.

274: A TALE ABOUT THE TIME

by CH Shih

By a vast spring barley field, I sat and read.

A little boy tapped on my shoulder. "Let's play hide-and-seek. You will be it."

The wind blew, the crops grew; I touched the ears of barley, and there he was in the distance, hiding.

"Ahoy, now I am sailing away."

Wave after wave off on a roll, rushing ashore.

I followed him and accidentally tripped into a rabbit hole, where I spotted a soft melting pocket watch. Beside it, a disappearing, wide smile adrift.

"Where do you want to go?"

I kept on falling. Caught a glimpse of a hanging mirror, wisps of white hair.

"There you are."

I woke up. By a vast barley field, I sat and listened to the ocean singing.

CH Shih's Biography

A cheerful mum that was 'made in Taiwan'. An IT programmer who loves literature alongside binary code. A person with passion for writing who hopes to share her love of nature with children by writing stories.

275: TOENAILS

by Gail Buffalo

"I know that is safe, but I can't go any further." Mama looked up after she peeled the top layer of nail from the top left half of my big toe. Then she peered at me with guarded eyes as if to say, "You should have known better."

I should have, but those rocks last spring were calling my name as I scrambled over one and then the next without proper footwear. Blood had long dried underneath my big toenails and now both were coming off.

At last they matched.

"That one will go soon," she added, nodding at the nail on my right foot's big toe. "You'll have to take care of the rest. I have to get dinner going," she lied, as she pressed the clippers to my chest.

Tonight was chilli night. There was nothing more to do except warm the bowls and shred the cheddar cheese. She just wanted to punctuate the weight of this problem and make it heavy enough that I'd never let it happen again.

Gail Buffalo's Biography

Gail left her native Appalachia to pursue urban education in 2001. In multiple literacy education and teacher training contexts, Gail connects with students by valuing and helping them leverage their unique, culturally situated strengths. She resides in New York City.

276: A PRISON OF MY OWN MAKING

by Laura Buckley

"Work from home," they said. "Experience complete freedom," they said.

I drift through endless bland days, watching other people live their busy, brightly-coloured lives outside my windows. I used to love to wake up and smell the coffee, specifically a takeaway coffee on the way to the office. Now, the smell follows me around my studio flat.

The carpet feels worn and tired beneath my bare feet; I haven't put socks on in weeks. Why would I? I have nowhere to go and no one to see.

"Is this that freedom they were banging on about?" I mutter aloud. The sound of my own voice, scratchy and under-used, comes as a surprise. It shouldn't. I haven't spoken to another human being in days.

The letters of my laptop keyboard click merrily as I type, yet another shout into the void, 'Anybody want to jump on a video call this afternoon?'

They're too busy, always so busy, and the disappointment is bitter. Or maybe that's just my over-brewed coffee.

Laura Buckley's Biography

Laura is an ex-teacher, now freelance writer and editor, who is thoroughly enjoying working 100% from home. Honestly. She puts out weekly writing advice and book reviews on her website (www.lauralizbuckley.net) and spends far too much time on Twitter.

277: DRIBBLE

by Jacqui Martin

The train lurched. To my horror, I had been resting my head on the man's shoulder next to me. I had dribbled. My breath smelt of garlic, masking my expensive primrose oil perfume.

His eyes were sparkling with amusement as he popped a mint into his mouth. He offered me one. I accepted, hoping to mask my bad breath.

All of a sudden there was this awful clang of metal and grind of the wheels on the track. My lukewarm coffee shot across, all over the lady opposite me. The rough material of the seat ripped into my tights.

I took a deep breath and looked at my fellow passenger; he was changing colour as he choked on his sweet. Another man hauled him out of his seat. I stood behind him and squeezed. Once, twice, and then put all my energy into the third thrust. It worked. The sweet shot out.

We both collapsed on the floor. I rested my head on his shoulder.

This time I didn't dribble, I laughed with relief.

Jacqui Martin's Biography

I'm new to fiction writing having written professional articles in the past. It's challenging and most of all inspirational. My study journey has been through a variety of distance learning opportunities. I'm also a member of the Suffolk Writers Group.

278: NOCTURNAL VISITS

by Glen Donaldson

At bedtime, I climbed into my squeaky iron bed, pulled the covers tight around my chin and lay there staring into the dark. I was all alone. Then there was a knock on the door.

"Can I come in?" moaned Grandpa's ghost.

"I guess so," I told him.

The temperature of my room grew suddenly cold, like arctic air. Grandpa's ghost sat on a creaky, wooden rocker by the door and rocked in the dark. The familiar smell of stale tobacco filled my nostrils. The clock on the wall ceased to tick.

By now, I was used to his visits. The first couple of times, I'd been scared and had called out to Great Auntie Cookie. But this was no ghoul, no phantom, no poltergeist. This was my dearest grandpa, the one who'd told me I was his favourite – though I wondered if he'd said that to all of us grandkids.

After he left, I stayed awake for a long time, listening to the sounds of the house.

Glen Donaldson's Biography

Glen Donaldson is an Australian hobby writer who blogs weekly and uniquely at both *Scenic Writer's Shack* and *Lost in Space Fireside*.

279: NO MEDIUM

by Jim Lemon

The train abruptly shudders off. Its mechanical twitch radiates through the packed bodies around me. Breath is inhaled or expelled, accompanied by muffled grunts, ahems and hums. Movement ripples and echoes in the crowd, random nudges quickly synchronised by the regular metallic thumping. Bound together by our numbers, the warm odours of my neighbours ooze into my nose as mine must into theirs. Recently applied scent invades my mouth, tickling my tongue.

   I wonder what babble of thoughts is chattering in the heads around me. Clues are offered in the squeaking and clicking that escapes their ear pieces, more explicit information in a mobile phone conversation. The infinite mystery of those inner worlds remains obscured. Are they revealed by mythic sensors operating within the white haired head on my left that diffuses a dried flower smell of age? She would know and answer my question if they were. We are gently squeezed together again in a parting embrace by our deceleration. The doors hiss open and we regain the illusion of independence.

Jim Lemon's Biography

Jim Lemon landed in Australia over 50 years ago and found that it suited him. He continues to enjoy the place even though both he and Australia have changed quite a bit in the interval.

280: TRAIN TERROR

by Bridget Yates

The train jerked into motion again; the strap hangers clutched each other to stay upright. I remained in my seat, clutching the blue bag for fear that it would fall. I was terrified, convinced that everyone somehow knew what I had done in callously and deliberately stealing the proceeds from the church fund-raiser.

There was a loud clang from underneath the carriage and I realised that there must be another problem. The other passengers groaned in frustration. I clutched the bag closer, running my hands over its rough surface; my nerves were at screaming pitch.

A strange, sweet smell began to waft through the carriage. Everyone involuntarily looked around. A little girl in a bright, primrose raincoat was sucking enthusiastically on a boiled sweet. Someone giggled. Soon everyone was laughing uncontrollably. I couldn't help myself and the blue bag, spewing out small change and raffle tickets, crashed to the floor with a rattling like a machine gun.

No more laughter.

Bridget Yates' Biography

I am a retired teacher who used to spend her pension on holidays and travel. Now, having had her wings clipped, she spends her time writing, reading, walking the dog and avoiding housework.

281: THE GREAT CAKE OFF

by Clare Tivey

I place my hands against the cool glass of the window and a splendour of sugar greets my dilating pupils. The candy pink, lemon yellow, dark chocolate and all that fluffy whipped cream. My mouth salivates but my inner voice screams, "Keep walking."

The Bridesmaid's dress is a rose-gold taffeta thing that rustles like a windy sail with every movement and uncomfortably squeezes my middle. Grabbing the fleshy tyre on my waist, feeling weak and tired, I am fed up, just not in the literal sense. With the exclusive smoothie diet and two HIIT sessions per week, I am losing pounds, just of the monetary kind.

Inside, seated by the window, I'm warm and cosy. Watching the bustling shoppers, I enjoy the background chatter and two large slices of cake, one a sticky, spicy ginger cake; the other a tangy lemon drizzle.

While inhaling the nutty aroma of the huge, full fat latte, I send a text.

'Sorry, I can't make the wedding plan meeting tonight, I think it was something I ate x'

Clare Tivey's Biography

I enjoy sniffing my partner's head, rowing my kayak through the rivers, the hoppy yet tropical flavour of a pale ale, the charming sight of the fox who visits for dinner each evening and loud, thrashy guitars.

282: BESSIE'S BREAD

by Deborah Rose Green

Bessie is making bread again. It's the third time this week and it's only Wednesday meaning she's either bored or in a really good mood. She thinks it's the latter, but she can't be sure. Just one more loaf, just one more.

Her little sister can't complain. She steps inside after a long school day and inhales deeply. Nothing can compare to the heart-warming, mouth-watering aroma of freshly baked bread. A backpack falls with a thud. The coat can stay on.

"This way I won't get crumbs on my uniform," Hannah argues when Mum complains. She throws the counter-height chair back and it screeches against the kitchen tiles.

"Hannah," Mum shouts, but Hannah isn't listening. Half a slice of warm bread is steaming in her hand and the rest is melting in her mouth. She savours the soft, crumbling heaven and gives Bessie a thumbs up.

"It tastes like happiness," she says, approving eagerly.

Bessie smiles. She's in a good mood, after all. "Mum, do you want a piece?"

Deborah Rose Green's Biography

Bessie is making bread again, much to the delight of her younger sister, Hannah, when she gets home from school. Seeing Hannah happy brings Bessie satisfaction.

www.instagram.com/authordeborahrose/

283: EARLY SUMMER WALK

by Duane L. Herrmann

Walking up the hill to my camping site, I stretch my legs as the last lap is steeper than the slope before. I am relieved my neighbour has moved his bait trap. He used rotting meat to lure the animals he is hunting to their deaths. The stench is attractive to them, but I could barely breathe. I don't agree with his actions, but there is no law against it.

As I walk higher, the wind begins to blow against my skin. Suddenly, I feel a tight little line across my chest, then it breaks. I've walked through another spider web anchor line. I have no choice, there is only one path.

Birds proclaim their territory and squirrels argue. Two butterflies weave into sight. They remind me of our own transformation: after death, we become glorious.

I swallow the last of an apple. It was old, near the end of last season's crop. I won't eat another until this fall's crop is in. They will again be crisp, sharp and exciting to my mouth.

Duane L. Herrmann's Biography

Duane L Herrmann survived an abusive childhood embellished with dyslexia, ADHD and now cyclothymia and PTSD. He knows whereof he writes. He grew up and remains on the Kansas prairie where breeze and trees calm him and help him write.

284: CHIC

by Nicole McIntosh

I started a new job – 'Handy Girl'.

Upon my arrival, my anxiety wore strong. All along my sleeve, I saw palpitations.

I knocked on the worn, dated, white door. I waited... An old, fragile lady answered, almost mirroring the door. She greeted me with pleasant, intrusive eyes.

As I entered, I saw that every position of time was displayed, forcing me to smell its memories.

I followed her into the living room and knew straight away that she had an animal. Small, thin hairs were scattered on an armchair. She had a Chihuahua called Charlie.

Each week, I'd do odd jobs proven too difficult for her and, each time, I'd hear a chapter about her life. A history of time that I would never experience.

I was eager with the knowledge of her yesterday, as she was of my today. Chic, her parents named her.

"Don't waste your life," she said.

How could I waste something I hadn't already obtained? She'd had her life, but I was only just starting mine.

Nicole McIntosh's Biography

Nicole McIntosh is a witty and inventive writer who is establishing herself within the creative field. Having written more than enough scripts and poems, and previously written for *True London*, Nicole is finally writing her own book, *My Friend ADHD*.
    www.koletoshwrites.com

285: AFTERWARDS

by John D Lary

In that moment, Stanley's world consisted of nothing but the high-pitched whine that the explosion had engendered in his shattered eardrums.

Being there, at the spot where the shell hit, the stink of cordite must have been overpowering, but Stanley had no sense of it. His vision had likewise shut down. No sense of smell, no sight.

Stanley smiled.

The fighting was, for him, now finished.

The noise in his head was unrelenting, but Stanley accepted it. Feeling began slowly to return to his body – not to his extremities, as those had been lost in the explosion, but to his neck, his back. The mud where he lay was a featherdown mattress. He snuggled down into it, feeling comfort such as he had been denied for countless months.

Despite his blindness, Stanley saw the woman as she approached across the muddy waste, her spotless white dress glowing brightly with a pure light.

She came directly to him and he looked into her face.

Then, cradled once again in her arms, Stanley knew he was safe.

John D Lary's Biography

John lives in Kent with his wife of 45 years. Although he is old enough to know better, John's grandchildren keep him feeling young.

286: THE ANGEL'S SWEET REFRAIN

by Linda Hibbin

Where's my knight in shining armour?

Always midnight. Mysterious scuffles, wind, rain, extreme cold, unbearable heat.

Crash, metallic squeak. My world transported.

Blinding light, multi-coloured, twinkling stars, faded flapping paper strips. Here we go again.

"My angel." No knight.

Familiar hands, scented with marzipan, straighten my tattered dress, brittle wings, caress my sparse locks.

Thick fruity smells mingle with brandy in the warm air. Children's favourites play in the background. "The king is in the altogether, the altogether... *whatever.*"

A finger wipes rosé across my lips, sweetening the stains from previous years.

She's wandering down memory lane. The ritual becomes shorter each year.

The artificial tree's a bundle of fun. Musty. More skeleton than foliage. Get this straight, there's no pleasure sitting up there with a metal spike stuck up my derrière.

Titillating conversation would pass the time but tree has turned from Jack the lad into grumpy old man. Deal with it, smelly, I do. What? I'm a grumpy old woman? Wait till I get on top of you.

Up I go. *Ouch.*

Linda Hibbin's Biography

Linda is a septuagenarian who has written stories for her granddaughter but became seriously hooked during lockdown by attending Zoom writing courses. She loves the challenge of flash fiction. Is more Pam Ayres than Tennyson when it comes to poetry.

287: THRILL OF THE COURT

by Jeniffer Lee

Glaring sunlight shines through the court, illuminating us like a spotlight and hurting my eyes.

Things to remember: straight platform, bent legs, eyes focused, razor-sharp. Reminding myself, I wait with bated breath, swallowing the taste of dust and old gym equipment. The scent of stale sweat reaches my nose, but it only makes me feel more alive.

I lift my feet off the ground by a millimeter. With a resounding, ear-splitting *CRACK*, the ball thunders across the net. A single pass close to the net gives a point to the other team.

"Aim for the next one," says my teammate, patting my back. Her fingers, like mine, feel rough and callused from practice.

Beep. I jump up like a bird, feeling my muscles coil, instantaneously imagining the scene where my spike is blocked and the point is lost.

I fiercely spike the ball with clenched teeth, feeling my nerves as the sound roars through the court. My fists connect, a sharp sting, then numbness.

The next moment, I open my eyes, cheers surrounding me.

Jeniffer Lee's Biography

Jeniffer Lee is a high school junior studying on Jeju Island, South Korea. She loves to read, write and play sports.

288: LEFT IN THE DARK

by Roger West

The train suddenly stopped inside a tunnel. It could only have been twenty minutes since we'd left the station. No one spoke and it felt rather creepy, everyone fidgeting, hoping for an explanation. A fellow traveller to my right reached into the breast pocket of their jacket, pulled out a silver cigarette holder, unsnapped a cigarette and blue tobacco smoke filled the air.

A clang from under the carriage. Had it been unhooked from the steam engine? At that moment, someone entered through the sliding door, a uniformed railway official perhaps, dressed in maroon with a yellow bow tie. He was rough around his unshaven, pasty features. Everyone turned in his direction, hoping for some explanation. As he passed me there was no sound, yet he gave off a sweet smelling aroma that disturbed the air. I recognised it immediately: Primrose. *How strange*, I thought, *for an old man.*

He moved, light-footed, to the opposite end of the carriage, raised an arm, then turned out the carriage lights...

Roger West's Biography

Hi there, I'm an ageing yet experienced sports/football writer/broadcaster/reporter/commentator wanting to venture into fiction as well as journalism. I have submitted two short stories for an anthology but not expecting too much.

289: SIGHT

by Anne Silva

He placed a hand on my arm.

I felt his warm hand on mine. Soft fingers, just rough on the tips from his constant guitar playing.

I turned my head in his direction. I could see his head of soft, wild curls and those brown eyes sparkling with endless happiness, which he always seemed to have in him.

"Such a beautiful day," he said. His voice was exactly like his touch. Soft, warm, musical. "The sun is shining down through the trees in bright white rays."

He lifted up my hand with his and placed it down on the soft grass, next to the cotton picnic blanket we were sitting on. I gasped as the blades of cold wet grass touched my hand.

"The grass is still wet with dew," he said. "It looks beautiful, just like you."

I felt my own lips curl in an involuntary, shy smile. I didn't know what beautiful was.

Happiness was radiating from me in almost tangible waves. He showed me everything my eyes could never see.

Anne Silva's Biography

Anne Silva is a student/writer from Kandy, Sri Lanka, who publishes her work online as Poetry of Despair. She is inspired by emotion and writes to express what she feels. You can read her work at:

www.instagram.com/Poetryofdespair

290: WHERE TIME FADES

by Adele Winston

In an ideal world, I'd be back there again. Pendine Sands at the height of summer, strolling along the warm beach barefoot. Drag my toe in the sand, write the children's names, the dog's name. We'll all wait and watch the tide come in, crawling, crawling lazily, licking the letters. Bubbles of froth hissing backwards with seaweed leaving shells behind, fresh and shined under the sun.

Then the seagulls squawk at the tide coming in. Fast. The waves are lapping my toes, sinking them in with the sand and pulling me in with its salty fizz. I'll let it reach my ankles. The cold of new water rising with every crash of wave.

There is a beauty in the sea crawling towards you, the boats on the horizon, the sun on your back, the smell of chips on the wind. When the slushy sound of the ice-cream van rolling along the beach reaches my ears, it's complete. I'm on holiday. There is laughter on the air. And the water is way past my ankles.

Adele Winston's Biography

Adele Winston is a Welsh author who was shortlisted for The Wells Festival of Literature and long listed for The Evesham Festival of Words and Crowvus Christmas Ghost Story Competition. She was awarded first prize at Crickhowell Women's Fest.

291: WAY TO GO TO MEET MY MAKER

by Fliss Zakaszewska

Phil Lynott blasting out 'Whisky in the Jar', me standing inches from the ten-foot speakers. I'm five-foot-nuffink, everyone else is at least six-foot-twelve as boozy breath and sweaty armpits power downwards. I take a slug from my bottle of almost cold beer and feel sick, my eardrums fit to burst.

Glass crunches underfoot as I bop along to 'Whisky in the Jar'. *Thank God for my Doc Martens*, I think, the sound of breaking glass reaching my ears above one-hundred-and-twenty decibels, beating even the mighty Lynott. Broken glass one, Lynott nil.

Isabel pokes me in the ribs. "You OK?" she mouths, then grabs my hand and leads me out.

Fresh air makes me reel as I look at her waving her arms, mouth opening and shutting, no sound coming out. *Either she's mad or I'm deaf*, I think as I start to fall…

…Everything's white, peaceful, and gentle music plays as a man in white leans over me and smiles.

"Worst case of tonsillitis I've ever seen, but you'll be fine soon, you'll be fine."

Fliss Zakaszewska's Biography

Born in Guatemala, Fliss has returned to her dad's homeland of Cornwall, UK. She'd write a ten-page essay when other kids wrote four. She's now learned both the meaning of the word 'brevity' and how it applies to her.
@FlissZak

292: SQUIRMING

by Ian Buzard

Her smile parted long enough to say something cool like, "What's up?" He felt like he was on stage; drenched in a white-hot spotlight and gouged by a thousand stares.

He tasted that morning's toast returning. He tried to relax his stance, but went too far and now he was staring. He snapped back up to her eyes, wondering how she could still be the same beauty after the thousand years this conversation had lasted. What was he even saying? Better check in.

"I love it when it's sunny, and stuff." Bravo. Is it possible to summon a heart attack and end this?

Her perfume, notes of jasmine and oud, a symphony evoking champagne beneath the smouldering ember of dusk. Or 'really nice' as he put it.

A panic alarm wailed in his skull and his brain initiated a self-destruct countdown.

"Maybe I'll see you here again tomorrow?" He knew full well they worked together in that very room and wondered if he did in fact just wink at her.

Ian Buzard's Biography

An aspiring screenwriter living in Glasgow. Writing short stories as often as possible to stay sane during these weird times.

293: WATERLOGGED BOREDOM

by Claris Lam

The train suddenly stopped.

Kelsey almost fell out of her seat, dropping her things. She winced at hearing a splash. As she straightened herself, she heard a bleary-voiced announcement: "Apologies for the stop… route will continue shortly."

She frowned, picking up her now-empty water bottle and her damp, blue romance book. It wasn't anything special, but she needed something to read to prevent boredom during her journey.

A sudden, loud clang echoed throughout the train and she briefly froze. Was the noise from the train tracks, or part of the train itself? Repairs in progress, possibly?

She peeked out from her row of seats, looking towards the other people in her carriage as she gripped onto her own seat, rough in her hands. One of them, a seated woman, heavily-perfumed with primrose, devoured sweet toffee.

Kelsey sighed and sank back into her own seat, wishing she hadn't spilled water on her book. She had no choice, now, but to watch everything around her, unless boredom overtook her.

Claris Lam's Biography

Claris Lam writes fiction, poetry and book reviews. Her poem, 'Paths', was published in *The Blank Page* in 2019. You can learn more about her work at:
www.mysticalauthoress.ca

294: HOME

by Seadeta Osmani

Snow melted, turning itself into a river of nothing,
   Winds are calling for fire,
   I am dreaming of you...

The candle burned away into darkness,
   The cat is peaceful,
   I am holding my heartbeat in the palm of my hand...

The call for prayer flashed through vast silence,
   Scent of jasmine reminded me of home,
   I surrender to you...

Seadeta Osmani's Biography

Seadeta Osmani – poet, translator, creative writer, dancer. Living and working in Zagreb, Croatia, writing poetry in both Croatian and English. One book of poetry self-published. Individual poems published in several collections of poetry internationally.
   www.facebook.com/s.o.poetrypoezija/

295: LOST WORLD

by Terence Waeland

From high in the bright green canopy of leaves, the throaty roar of a howler monkey assaults his sensitive ears. Through the dense foliage, luminous shafts of sunlight glow white in the rising jungle mist. He turns his head, looking for some sign of a path through the tangled tendrils hanging from the tall, glistening trees.

Buzzing mosquitoes swarm all around, forcing him to hold his breath for fear of swallowing any of the nasty little insects. His hands are sweaty and his shirt sticks to his clammy chest. He runs his tongue across his salty lips; although desperate to reach out for his bottle of cool, cool water, he doesn't dare move his arms.

The nutty aroma of hot coffee wafts past his nostrils, just as a piercing chime shatters the still air. He stands up immediately and removes his VR headset in time to hear the announcement: "We are now approaching London Waterloo Station. Please make sure you take all your belongings with you when leaving the train."

Terence Waeland's Biography

I'm a graphic designer, living in Kent, and close to finishing my second novel. Still unpublished, previous submissions have reached the top thirty of the London Short Story Prize and the semi-finals of the Screencraft Cinematic Short Story Writing Competition.
www.facebook.com/twaeland

296: ANIMAL INSTINCT

by Theresa Ryder

We crouched under smoking palm leaves. Night-ticking crickets close in the oily air. A swollen moon glanced on ground humps that I prayed were sleeping cattle. In the dank darkness a stranger's fist squeezed my heart, held my breath, wet my cheeks. I licked the metal fug of blood from my lip, scent to animals, and hugged the rough handle. The blade at my ear orange-licked in reflected fire. Twitching, I pushed up. Muscle and instinct urged me forward. My heart punching.

"Be still, child. Hush."

His heavy hand on my shoulder. His panting breath warm on my ear. His smell of burning rubber, sweat, gunpowder, was not his smell. I wanted him to play. Like humans again, close in mock wrestling, knees bent, circling wide his bear-like arms. Or pushing me on the roped tyre hung over the dry river, my head flung back, laughing.

Now my duty was to be still. Silent. Hunker low. Swing my blade.

Theresa Ryder's Biography

Theresa is a writer and teacher. Her first short story submission won the Molly Keane Creative Writing Award and she has been published widely since. She is a contributor to *The 32: An Anthology of Working Class Voices*, (May 2021).

@TheresaRyder_

297: TUESDAY MORNING

by Jade Swann

A series of pops strike the air like firecrackers, breaking up the dismal tapping of keys. My spine shudders in gratitude as I twist the other way, stretching the stiff ligaments as far as they'll go. The cracked leather of my chair squelches as I settle back into it.

I sip my coffee. Tepid, the milk lukewarm. It slides down my throat and sits uncomfortably cool in my chest. My mouth twitches at the bitterness, the sugar settled into a grainy mess at the bottom of the flimsy paper cup. I stir it, wincing as the thin plastic stick crunches and grinds the tiny granules.

My lungs breathe in the stale atmosphere and release it with a low sigh.

Only three more hours until lunch.

Jade Swann's Biography

Jade Swann can be found writing with a cup of coffee in one hand and a Boston terrier by her side.
www.jade-swann.com

298: LOVE FROM RUIN

by Jessica Ann George

"Johnny," she said. "Did you do this?" Her voice, although soft, rang in my ears. I couldn't believe what I'd done... neither could she.

I ruined the loving memory of her husband and I felt her heart wither away. A single mother and a disobedient son. I felt so much pain... my heart stopped. All the nights before, I left her alone, going off to parties where I broke every rule my mum ever instilled in me, and tonight I felt the shame.

Looking down, there were several shards of glass. Among them, a small rose, kept in memory of my dad the day he passed away. But so fragile, it was torn apart.

Kneeling, I began gathering the glass pieces. They cut deep into my skin, blood all over them. She offered me a clean, yellow glove, but I refused. I deserved to feel the agony.

Bending down, tears running down my cheeks, I could faintly smell the rose. I felt the sweet love that my parents had for me. I got up and hugged her, love I'd never shown before.

Jessica Ann George's Biography

I am a very passionate baker (although some taste my food with a dash of dread), writer, coder and LEGO Enthusiast. Reading comics and the classics are also interests of mine, alongside playing Jim Croce on my acoustic guitar.

299: RECIPE BY THE NOSE

by A S Winter

This was the most unusual food festival: Recipe by the Nose. There was only one rule: participants had to taste as many varieties of dishes as they could. The response had been overwhelming and emergency services had been called in to rein in any possible mishap.

What's the catch? everyone in the crowd wondered. It was revealed when the host came on the stage among thunderous applause.

The host announced that the chefs were blindfolded while cooking the dishes and they could only use their sense of smell to select the ingredients. The crowd fell silent. Everyone's horrible experience with food crept into their minds. Some called it quits, but many overcame their fear and went ahead for tasting.

The first hour was exciting but then disaster followed. People started complaining about stomach ache, pain and many fainted. Emergency services were swift in their response and sick people were moved to hospital.

'Don't Follow Your Nose' and 'Knocked by Surprise' were news headlines the next morning.

A S Winter's Biography

A S Winter works as a researcher in his day job and when he is not working he uses his imagination and creativity to write flash fictions and stories.

300: PINK

by Caroline Ryder

"It's going to be OK, you'll like it here," she keeps saying, but I do not want to be here. Eyes shut tight they cannot see me.

Talking, laughing, crying, shouting, different strange voices, music, loud bangs, soft rustles, clicks, it hurts my ears.

Smells different, strange smells, I like that sweet one.

I open one eye slowly. They don't see me. I see them, lots of them, big and small, constant moving, lights, colours everywhere, sunlight through the window. I move.

They keep talking, that sweet, nice smell is nearby. Shiny, sparkly and pink. I like pink. If I reach slowly, I can touch it, poke, squeeze, squidgy, squish, it moves in my fingers, it smells so good, I like jelly. Just a little bite, ugh, yuck, spitting and crying, not jelly.

"Mummy," I shout.

Now she sees me. "It's OK, Mummy is here."

The person with the pink top crouches down. "It's playdough, not to eat." She smiles. "Hello, Katie. You will like it here at nursery," she says.

I like pink.

Caroline Ryder's Biography

An Irish woman living in London. Wife and mother to three adults. A passion for working in Childcare led to a career teaching in Further and Higher Education. Lockdown reminded me to do something creative I enjoy doing like writing.

A FINAL NOTE

Allen and I would like to say one last raucous THANK YOU to all the authors featured in this anthology. Their generosity is helping support a very worthy charity and it's an honour to present their stories in this collection.

Don't forget to check my website for more writing challenges. You will be able to find all the details here: www.christopherfielden.com/writing-challenges/

There is also an 'Authors of the Flash Fiction Writing Challenges' Facebook group that runs its own regular challenges. It's open to everyone. Please feel free to join here:
www.facebook.com/groups/157928995061095/

I will say farewell Bristol-style:

Cheers me dears,

Chris Fielden

Printed in Great Britain
by Amazon